BRUNSWICK

KURT DYER, JR.

ISBN
978-1-958690-40-6 (Paperback)
978-1-958690-41-3 (eBook)
978-1-958690-39-0 (Hardcover)

TABLE OF CONTENTS

CHAPTER 1

It was barely eight thirty in the morning when the storm began to roll in on that fairly warm Monday in August. Tom Brunswick had just begun putting the finishing nails in the last of the shingles on the roof of his new house. A house in which he had been building on now for nearly two years. It had been something he and his wife, Annie, had been dreaming of doing since the day they had decided to marry nearly five years earlier.

The house stood a towering two stories high and held four complete bedrooms upstairs. Enclosing the front end of the house, Tom had built a horseshoe shaped porch that stretched to four feet on either side of the house and stood about two feet off the ground. Concealed behind the steps was the base wall in which a twelve-foot-deep basement rested beneath the house.

Inside; three of the bedrooms were designed with a perfect eighteen square feet of dimensions. This would allow a full-size bed, a bureau, a night stand, a reading desk with chair, and still have enough room to fit three to five kids comfortably on the floor with room enough to play. Tom built these rooms with the same dimensions for one reason only. If children were born in the near future, there would be no bickering over who would get the bigger room.

The fourth bedroom was designed with dimensions of twenty-four square feet, allowing room for a couple of reading chairs with stands and a lamp beside each, a king size bed with nightstands on either side, a bureau, and a vanity for Annie. The only other room that occupied the upstairs was a full bathroom equipped with a claw-footed tub, sink, and toilet and was connected only to the master bedroom.

The first floor of the house held a huge foyer in which a staircase lay to the right of the entrance with another bathroom fit just under the staircase, a long hallway that led to the back of the house and to another entrance to a huge dining room to the left. From the dining room, the next room over was a huge kitchen where Annie enjoyed cooking and baking. To the right of the foyer was a living area with a door at the end of the room leading into a private library. Being a carpenter in his off time and a fisherman in his work life, Tom loved to read just as his wife did, and managed to keep quite a collection of books of all different subjects.

The set up of the house could almost be considered a mansion with the amount of space each room allowed but it was simply for décor more than anything. Both of them always dreamed about having a huge house with room to have everything they ever wanted. This house was a result of their dreams and all their hard work in making it come true.

Coming down from the roof just as the first raindrops hit the top of his head, Tom took the ladder away from the house and placed it in a shed to the rear of the property and then went inside. Almost immediately upon stepping through the front door it began to downpour.

"Get the roof finished?" Annie asked as she walked in by way of the kitchen and dining room.

"Yeah finally; just in time by the sounds of it." He said as he took his hat off and placed it on the coat/hat rack beside the entranceway. "What's for lunch? It smells great."

"Beef stew. It'll be ready in about half an hour."

"Good, I'll go take a bath and shave." Tom said, making his way up the stairs to their bedroom for clothes to change into. He had been working on the roof since five that morning and had not given himself the luxury of getting a bath or a shave until he was done.

Deciding to use the bathroom downstairs instead of the one connected to their bedroom, Tom headed back down the stairs. He wanted to be sure he could hear Annie call when lunch was ready.

Before entering the bathroom, he hollered out to his wife who had returned to the kitchen, "I love you!"

"I love you too!" She called back.

* * *

Returning to the kitchen, Annie began to stir the pot containing the stew when a knock came at the front door. "Now who in the world could that be?" She whispered to herself, wiping her hands on her apron and making her way back to the foyer to answer the door.

The knocking continued growing in tone to more of a pounding by the time she reached the door. "Hold on hold on, I'm coming!" She hollered out as she peered through the side glass onto the porch. A man stood outside the door drenched from head to toe and continued to pound on the door.

The cell doors opened all at once as the full-time residents of the Maine State Prison were let out of their cells for work detail. Jacob Frost, currently serving a life sentence for the rape and murder of two women in Kennebec County, had already served five years of his sentence and had earned himself a spot on a work crew that consisted of five other men. Their job was to work on the railroad line coming through the fisherman's town of Rockland; only five miles up the road. He had worked as a member of this crew for over four months now and felt that he had earned a little bit of leeway with the guards that were assigned to monitor them.

There were no '*Chain Gangs*' in the state of Maine but they *were* heavily guarded and monitored whenever they went outside the gates of the prison. But before leaving the front gates, each of them were shackled in what the guards called 'four-point restraints. This, of course, meant that shackles were placed on their wrists and ankles with a chain wrapped around their waists and another chain attached to that, linking the two shackles so that the only way they could move was to take baby steps. Once they arrived at their destination, they were released from their restraints and herded together between guards on different sections of a perimeter to discourage escape.

Jacob had been planning his escape from this wretched facility since the day he walked through the doors. He had monitored all of the guards from dawn to dusk, watching everything they did and taking mental notes of their daily habits that might help him when the time came. He decided today was the day to put all his planning into action.

Knowing that he and the other prisoners would be strip searched individually of each other before exiting their cell block, Jacob dared not try to hide a weapon on his person but instead managed to stash one that he had been making at the job site. It was a limb of a tree that he had broken down to four to five inches long. He had been slowly sharpening down one point of his weapon using a jagged stone he had found near the tracks on his first day of his work detail. When it was to the sharpness he wanted, he managed to tuck it under the wheel-well of the back tire of the truck the guards used to transport them.

Once he and the others had been thoroughly searched, Jacob walked to the back of the truck where he waited for the guards to place the shackles on his wrists and ankles. When the time came for his shackles to be placed, he waited anxiously for them to have him put his hands on the truck for support while they placed the shackles on his ankles from behind. When the order came, he obliged with a smile painted across his face.

Raising one foot behind him, the guard assigned to shackle him grabbed hold of the back of his shirt and secured the shackle. When Jacob was told to put that one down and to lift the other foot, he obliged but stumbled forward as though he had lost his balance. As he caught himself on the wheel-well, he grabbed his weapon.

"Get up!" The guard shouted from behind him.

Quickly putting his unshackled foot on the ground, he pivoted and pushed the make-shift weapon into the guard's neck.

Before either the other prisoners or the remaining four guards could react to what he had just done, Jacob pulled the weapon from the dead guard's throat and snatched the first guard that came at him pressing the point of the make-shift weapon against the guard's temple and said, "If any of you try anything, this pig's dead too."

From the direction of the nearest wall watchtower came the sound of shotgun fire but the rounds missed him and plunged into the dirt three feet away. Turning his human shield to face the gunner he shouted, "I mean it! Drop the gun or this pig's dead!"

The guard on the wall did as he was instructed, reluctantly, as a man wearing a Captain insignia came walking out of the main building with his hands raised high in the air. "Calm down! Calm down!" He said as he approached.

Pressing firmer with the shank against the guard's temple, Jacob said, "Every one of you back off!"

Motioning for his men to follow his lead, the captain began stepping backward toward the door and his men followed as did the other prisoners for Jacob had made it clear to them as well that they were not welcome in his plans.

"Open the gates!" Jacob shouted.

"We can't do that." The captain said in a firm but calm voice.

"If you want this pig to see his family tonight, you will." Jacob said, pushing harder and a small trickle of blood escaped around the point of the weapon and began making its way down the side of the guard's neck.

With a wave of the captain's hand, the gate began to open. Jacob told his hostage to give him the keys to the truck but the man hesitated a little trying to find the captain with his eyes. When Jacob twisted the point into his temple causing a little more blood to trickle out of his wound, he said, "They're in the truck."

Pulling his hostage with him, Jacob got behind the wheel and then slid over, pulling his hostage in with him and ordered him to drive. Giving the guard a little leeway, he watched carefully as the guard put the truck into gear and the vehicle bucked into first gear and drove out of the gate.

* * *

Reaching the small fisherman's town of Rockland, Jacob told the guard to pull over when he spotted a fishing supply store on the right just after entering the town.

"That'll do nicely." Jacob said, focusing his attention back to the guard.

"What're you gonna do?" The guard asked terrified of what was to come next.

"You won't have to worry about that." Jacob said as he pressed hard and firm with his shank against the guard's throat, now puncturing the skin deep. As the guard began to flop in the front seat, trying to fight his way out of Jacob's grasp, he opened the door and fell out of the truck.

Getting out of the truck himself, Jacob pushed harder against the embedded shank and the last gasp of breath escaped the fallen guard's lips. Jacob picked up the corpse as through it was nothing but a cord of wood, and flung the body into the bed of the truck.

Knowing that it had to be late enough in the morning for the store to be open, Jacob stepped to the door and pushed lightly on the glass and the door opened. Stepping through the threshold, he walked up to a counter and began to look over the many hunting and fishing knives that the clerk had in the case.

"May I help you sir?" A man said approaching him from the left.

"Yeah, I want this one." Jacob said, pointing at a hunting knife with a seven-inch blade from hilt to tip.

"Excellent selection sir; only a hundred dollars."

"I was thinking a little lower."

"How much are you looking to spend sir? Maybe I can help you find something else."

"No, I want that one." Jacob persisted.

"Sir, I can't go down on the price."

"No one said you had to." Jacob said, reaching across the counter and grabbing hold of the back of the clerk's head and quickly slamming it down hard against the top of the glass casing, breaking the man's head open as well as the casing at the same time.

"Thank you. Don't mind if I do." Jacob said, pulling the bleeding man's head out of the case and reaching in with his free hand to claim his prize.

With his new weapon in hand, he came around the counter and plunged the blade into the man's sternum and yanked up hard. The final gasps of breath escaping the man told Jacob that he had made a good choice.

* * *

Back in the truck with his new knife tucked securely behind him, Jacob started the truck and headed north along Route 1 just as the first rain drops began to fall against the windshield signaling a huge storm making its way in. The smile on his face grew larger as he knew that his chances of escaping successfully had just risen in odds.

Careful to obey the speed limit so as to not bring unwanted attention to himself, he continued along Route 1, following it north as the rain picked up in intensity. By the time the police caught on to the direction he was taking, he would already be gone.

Within twenty miles, just on the other side of Rockport on Route 1, Jacob pulled off the main highway and traveled a dirt road until the truck began to sputter, signaling that he was quickly running out of gas.

Abandoning the truck along the side of the dirt road, he entered a driveway that led him up a steep incline and around a bend to the entrance of a huge house sitting atop the hill.

With his new toy now in hand, Jacob made his way up the muddy road to the house and stepped up to the door where he knocked relentlessly. Within a matter of minutes, a woman answered.

The rain pounded against the ground so hard that it splashed four to six inches off the ground when it hit, forming puddles on the lawn outside. With the darkness of the rain, it was extremely difficult to see anything outside.

As Annie opened the door to greet the soaked stranger outside her door, she was suddenly struck with a huge hand across her head knocking her to the floor. Stunned, she slowly began to lift herself from the floor in an effort to call for her husband, but was stopped short when the man entered and dropped his entire weight down onto her chest, knocking what little wind she had in her completely out.

Maneuvering his body down a few inches to where he was straddling her stomach now, the man withdrew a huge knife from behind his back. With his free hand, he covered Annie's throat and squeezed so hard that it restricted the circulation of blood and air to her brain. Darkness quickly overtook her.

* * *

With knife in hand, Jacob began cutting away the woman's clothing piece by piece from her body and threw them this way and that until she was wearing only her underwear. In the background, Jacob could hear running water which told him that most likely the man of the house was using the bath.

When the woman was completely unconscious, Jacob relinquished his grip on her throat, picked her now near naked body from the floor, and carried her over his shoulder to the staircase.

At the top of the stairs, he lay her body on the floor and took his knife from the waistband of his pants where he had returned it earlier. He plunged the blade into her stomach, savagely tearing into the tissue and bringing her instantly back to consciousness for no more than a second – long enough for one last gasp of air – before succumbing once again to darkness's hold on her. This time, however, she would never wake again.

Deciding to leave a nice little present for the man of the house, Jacob proceeded to cut the woman from belly to breast, releasing her life force into the blood flow. Like water from a spigot, it trickled down the staircase little by little until it formed a small puddle at the base of the stairs. Though he knew the woman was dead, Jacob slit her throat from one end to the other, finishing his work.

From her lifeless body, Jacob took refuge in the first bedroom he came to and awaited the man of the house to find the gift he had left for him, and to feel the gift he still had waiting.

* * *

It took Tom exactly fifteen minutes to take his bath, mainly because he enjoyed sinking under the water to allow the warmness of the water to sooth his aching muscles. He loved to relish in its purity and warmth. It never failed to replenish all energy drained by a hard day's work; even though today's work lasted only a couple of hours.

He toweled himself and dressed into a pair of jeans, a flannel shirt, and a fresh clean pair of white cotton socks. Exiting the bathroom door, he could hear his stomach calling for some of Annie's delicious beef stew.

"Dinner ready hon?" He called out as he stepped into the foyer from the bathroom's light. He became frozen in place at the sight of Annie's clothes lying on the floor just inside the doorway.

At first, he thought that maybe she wanted dessert before the meal and this was her way of telling him so. He walked over to the clothes, calling her name low but audible. He bent down to study the clothes more closely and noticed that this wasn't some erotic game that his wife might be playing. His wife's clothes had not been taken off her body purposely by herself; they had been cut and ripped off. Realizing that something was deadly wrong, he dropped the clothes to the floor and began calling his wife's name louder and louder as he frantically searched the house, beginning in the kitchen.

"Annie! Annie! Annie!"

As worry began to creep inside his chest, Tom began making his way from the kitchen, into the dining room, and back into the foyer. His destination was now the living room and the library. He hoped against hope that she had somehow escaped her attacker and was hiding somewhere in the house. He was also hoping against hope that her attacker had left without doing any more damage.

As he was passing the staircase, he noticed something dark on the floor at the base of the stairs. At the sight of it, he didn't want to admit what he was seeing. He shook his head back and forth telling himself, "No… no… no…"

His slowly raised his eyes from the puddle at the base of the stairs and followed each step to the top where he found what he had been dreading. Annie's motionless body lay at the top of the stairs.

Climbing the steps two at a time, careful not to step into the blood, Tom reached the body of his wife and scooped her into his arms. All other thoughts completely escaped his mind as he held her lifeless head in his lap. His whole world had just crashed around him in one instant. His entire reason for living was now lying lifeless in his arms.

After several minutes of crying over her beautiful face, he gently placed her head back down to the floor. He stood and went into their bedroom, which was the first one on the left, in order to retrieve a blanket to cover her with until the police could arrive. The police would be his next step. He needed to phone them as soon as possible, but first, he needed to cover Annie.

Stepping into the bedroom, he took three steps toward the bed when he felt someone grab him from behind. A second later, he was in the air and landing across the bed.

* * *

After grabbing the surprised man by the scuff of his shirt and by the seat of his pants, Jacob launched him across the room to where he landed atop the bed.

As the man turned over to see his attacker, Jacob sank his knife into the man's side, aligned perfectly with his kidneys, and twisted. Withdrawing it for a second run through, Jacob smiled when the man screamed in pain, but his smile quickly darkened when the man kicked him in the gut and away from the bed.

As Jacob collected himself, he watched the man get up from the bed, holding his wound with his left hand, and ran out of the room. Jacob quickly gave chase as he followed the man out of the room. Believing that his prey was on his way to a phone to call the police, Jacob was surprised to find the man sitting at his wife's side at the head of the stairs with her head in his lap once more.

He had watched from the bedroom when the man had found his wife and done this exact same thing. He had smiled at the sight of his work. Now, however, he wasn't smiling. Lifting the knife over his head, determined to run it through the man's chest to finish the job, Jacob was surprised yet again when the man grabbed hold of both his legs with one arm and pulled him off his feet, causing him to plummet down the stairs. He tried to catch himself many times and stop the roll but he only managed to clobber every peg holding up the banister to the left of the wall connected to the staircase.

When he neared the bottom of the stairs, he felt something crack in his neck. When he finally came to a stop, he felt darkness overtake him and he closed his eyes to it.

* * *

Although he knew that he should get up and call the police, Tom could not get his body to cooperate. Instead of getting to his feet, he held strong to Annie's head as it rested in his lap. He was determined that if he was going to die, it would be with her in his arms.

As the room around him began to grow darker and darker, he felt the room grow cold and then his eyes growing heavy. He couldn't stop himself from closing them no matter how hard he tried. Soon, he relented to the weight and allowed his lids to close. Death came quickly to gather his final breath.

* * *

Two hours later, Jacob opened his eyes at the bottom of the staircase. His head throbbed as did his neck and nearly every other bone in his body. Gently lifting his aching head from against the wall, Jacob was rewarded instantly with a sharp intense pain shooting along his neck. Getting to his feet, Jacob stumbled away from the staircase and down the hallway immediately to his right. He turned into the dining room and quickly found himself in the kitchen within another ten feet. With his knife still in hand, he opened the back door and stumbled into the back yard.

He was only a hundred yards from the house when he nearly fell over, and in the process of catching his balance; he dropped his newly acquired friend into the grass. Feeling too much pain to bend over to retrieve it, Jacob stumbled his way into the wooded perimeter of the property.

Five hundred yards... six hundred yards... now seven hundred yards from the house, Jacob could travel no further. Leaning against a tree, he closed his eyes and soon thereafter he could no longer feel the pain. He could no longer feel the rain still falling atop him. He could no longer feel his body. All there was now... was darkness.

With thunder rolling in the background as though God himself was bowling with his angels, rain beating so hard against the ground that each drop cascaded a wave of water from the ground at least four to six inches, and lightning skipping from cloud to cloud, illuminating the night and lighting a backdrop to a huge house that stood two stories high. Huge black birds circled above the house and cawed from the trees. No other sight could be scarier.

The house stood atop a hill set back deep into the woods of some very tall and eerie trees. With each flash of lightning, the house gave off a clearer image. A porch, beginning to rot away, still embraced the front end of the house like a horseshoe. Steps led to the front porch from the dirt driveway; they too were rotting away. Tall grass, nearly five feet high, circled the entire house, but the front door became the center of attention. Emanating from the door came a loud and insistent pounding seemingly drawing closer and closer. Suddenly the door began to open…

The sound of the alarm clock buzzing annoyingly loud quickly woke Samantha Elliot from her reoccurring nightmare of over three weeks straight. She didn't know exactly what it was about this house that plagued her dreams and frightened her so much. As far as she knew, she had never been there before. It was as if something was calling her – drawing her – to that house. Problem was; she had no idea if it even existed outside her nightmare. Even if it did exist, she had no way of knowing where it was located; and if she did know or could find it, she had no intension of going there.

Pulling herself out of bed even as she was turning off her insistent alarm clock, Samantha switched on the bedside lamp and made her way into the bathroom. It was six thirty in the morning and she needed to get ready for work. The bad guys never rested so neither could she. Grabbing a pair of slacks, a turtleneck sweater, and some undergarments, she went into the bathroom to take a shower with the events of her dream still playing in her mind.

She was in the shower only five minutes when the phone beside her bed began to ring. She didn't have to get out of the shower to know who was calling and when the machine picked up; her assumption proved correct.

Dan Riley had been her partner for nearly six years now and was like a father to her. Hell, he was old enough to be her father. And he never grew tired of letting her know that either. "Rise and shine Valentine! We got bad guys to catch and torment and as much fun as it would be; I don't really want to do it all on my own. So, get those beautiful buns of yours out of that bed and get down here so we can have some fun."

Ignoring the call, she continued her mesmerizing shower. Allowing the water to engulf her body into its power and purity; she arched her back to let it flow through her hair and then relaxed her back as it gave a gentle massage from one end of her back to the other. After lathering up and rinsing off, she was in the middle of putting her final rinse of conditioner in her hair when the phone rang again.

"This is strange." She said to herself. She knew that Dan never called twice, unless of course it was urgent. Quickly washing the conditioner from her hair and turning off the water just in time to hear the beep sound on her machine for the caller to leave a message.

"Sgt. Elliot? This is Captain Ford; I need you in the station immediately and in my office." The voice said; then hung up.

"Shit! I wonder what he wants." She said as she got out of the tub and grabbed a towel to dry off.

When she was thoroughly towel dried, she wrapped the towel around her naked body, tucking the end of it between her breasts to keep it in place, and went back into her bedroom to get dressed. Once satisfied with her apparel, she went back into the bathroom and blow dried her long blonde hair and then brushed it out. Grabbing a black scrunchie from the sink counter, she tied her hair back into a tight ponytail and returned to her bedroom to gather her equipment.

With badge firmly fastened to her belt and sidearm in place, she looked at the full-length mirror attached to her closet door and decided that she looked professional enough. Turning off the bedside lamp, she grabbed her keys from the table beside the front door as she left her apartment and headed for her car.

* * *

"Alright Dan, I got her. She should be on her way. Just what do you boys have planned?" Captain Ford said as he hung up the phone.

"Oh, we figured we'd take her over to Jackie's Place for some real R & R. She's been so wound up lately, she probably forgot today was her birthday." Dan said.

"Well, as long as I have somebody here while you five do this, I don't suppose I mind. She deserves a day off. Lord only knows when she had one last."

* * *

It was a quarter after seven when Samantha walked into the station house. Concerned with what the captain might want so early in the morning, yet at the same time, not really worried. She knew she wasn't late for work; her shift really didn't start until eight and it normally lasted until well into the midnight hours. Deciding to take the stairs instead of the elevator, she made it to the homicide division's floor in record time, only to find that there were only a few other people there.

As she made her way to Captain Ford's office, the skeleton crew gave quick glances in her direction and some even said "Good Morning" as she passed them. When she arrived at Captain Ford's door, all of them fell completely silent. If a pin dropped in this room, everyone three doors down could easily hear it.

The blinds in his office were all closed and she paused before opening the door. She couldn't hear any sounds coming from within nor could she see any lights on under the door. Curious, she turned the knob and opened the door, reaching for the light switch at the same time as entering the room. "Captain?" She said as the light came on.

From behind, someone grabbed her, pinning her arms to her side. Then they covered her eyes. This someone was very strong, because she could hardly put up much of a struggle. As she continued to squirm to try and free herself, something went over her head just as the big man let go, only to grab her again before she could react to his release.

"Alright Dan, I know that's you. You better let me go before I kick your ass up between your eyeballs. I'm not kidding! Dan! Dan! Let me loose!" She cried out as the person holding her continued to hold on tight.

"Okay boys, grab her legs. Let's get her to the car." A very recognizable voice said from behind her.

"Dan, you're soooo asking for it now. Whatever you've got planned, don't even think about it!"

"Settle down Kid, it's about time you got a break and you're going to get one even if we gotta hog-tie you and drag you outta here. In fact, that's exactly what we're going to do." Dan said as he loosened his grip on her.

'Kid' is what Dan had called her since she arrived at the precinct. Everyone gave her a hard time not only because she was a rookie detective but mainly, she felt, because she was a woman. Dan was the only one who befriended her at first. She didn't mind being called 'Kid' by him. After all, he was twenty years older than she and she was only twenty-seven.

"I'm not telling you again Dan. You better let me go!" She demanded.

"Good. Cause quite frankly I'm tired of hearing it. Now just be quiet and relax."

She squirmed as much as she could just because he told her not to as they carried her outside and put her inside a vehicle. Once she heard the doors close, they finally let her go and took the blanket from over her head; the blanket had done little to contain her flailing limbs as she kicked at them.

"Whoa there, Kid." Dan said trying to calm her.

She looked around the car and realized she was in some sort of limousine and there were four others with Dan sitting beside her; Bruce Clayton, Robert McKinney, Jack Payne, and Bill Goat, whom everyone amply called "Billie Goat".

Starting with Dan, she leaned forward in her seat and punched each of them in the arm. "Now, where are you taking me you assholes?" She said as she sat back into her seat.

"Oww! You know, for a little shit, you sure pack a wallop."

"And don't you forget it! Now where the hell are you taking me?"

"Hey, we're entitled to surprise you."

"Who says?"

"Well, at least I am." Dan said.

"Who says?" She repeated.

"Well, I'm going to anyway. You'll just have to wait and see."

"I can tell you right now, I'm not gonna like it."

"Give it a chance, Kid."

* * *

Three hours later, they stopped for gas. The limo driver got out and pumped. Samantha looked out the window and said, "Alright; enough's enough. Where're you takin' me?"

No answer.

When the gas was pumped and the bill was paid, they were off again. Without a clue where they were going and nothing, she could do about it, she decided to go ahead and make the best of it.

She tried just shooting the breeze but it just made her want to shoot each one of them instead, so she said nothing and just sat back in the seat and waited.

Within another hour, the silence was too much for Dan to bear. "Are you really that angry, Kid?"

No answer.

"Would it make you feel better if I told you where we're going?"

"It might." She sulked.

"Alright, you win this battle. I'm sure you've forgotten what day it is, but we haven't. We're taken you out for your birthday. The captain gave us all the day off. My sister has a bar over in Kansas City called Jackie's Place; that's where we're going."

"Why the hell would you take me so far just to go to a bar?"

"Well, one reason is to get you as far away from work as possible. Another is… well… look at what time it is. I mean, we left the station around seven thirty; it's now a little after eleven thirty. By the time we get there, it'll be around three or four o'clock."

"Yeah, and it'll be morning before we get back. What are we going to do tomorrow with a hangover and nauseated stomachs trying to work?"

"The captain knows where we're going and what we're doing so I'm sure he'll understand if we're not a hundred percent tomorrow. So, Sam… Kid… Stop worrying. And for God's sake, stop making excuses not to go."

"You know I'm gonna kill you, don't you?"

* * *

At four fifteen they arrived in Kansas City, within another fifteen minutes the limousine pulled into the parking lot of a small tavern with the name JACKIE'S PLACE in neon letters above the front door. As Samantha and the rest of the "partygoers" exited the back of the limo, she looked around at the tiny bar and then at Dan with a look that could kill.

"I can't believe you stuffed me in an oversized car and dragged me six hours across state, or I should say to another state, for this… this dump."

"Trust me Kid; it's more than what it seems. Let's go in." Dan said as he put his hand on her shoulder. "Oh, by the way Kid, I don't think you'll need that." He said pointing down to her gun.

"Maybe, maybe not, but I take my gun everywhere, you know that."

"I know, I know. Whatever makes you feel better Kid."

"Thank you; now let's get this over with." Samantha said as she took the lead to enter the bar.

Inside was nothing like the outside. Walking through the door, she stopped and looked around. A fifteen-foot-long bar sat directly inside the door, a closed in hallway at the end of the bar lead to restroom areas.

A door behind the bar led to a room in the back that, considering the sign on the wall behind the bar that read BAR AND GRILL, told her that the room was most likely a kitchen. A huge mirror rested along the wall behind the bar so that the bartender could keep a close eye on everyone behind her.

Several varieties of liquor bottles lined the shelves in front of the mirror. Along the front of bar were stools with padded seat cushions atop them. Along each wall were booths to sit at. Four pool tables rested in the center of the room with people currently playing. Off to one side was a dance floor approximately six feet by ten and a sliding partition directly across the room that had a sign above it that read PRIVATE.

Other than the three or four other patrons at the bar and two guys playing pool, the place was virtually empty. "C'mon guys, this way to the party." Dan said as he took the lead to the partitioned wall.

Sliding the partition open enough for them to slip inside, Samantha saw several tables put together in the center of the room. A tablecloth, which hung to the floor, draped over the table. In one corner stood a big screen television, to the side of that was a karaoke machine that looked as if it was hooked up to the TV, in the other corner was a C.D. jukebox, and there was a large banner draped across the back wall that read HAPPY BIRTHDAY KID!

"You know, I'm gonna kill you." Samantha repeated as she looked over and up at Dan.

"Yeah, yeah, whatever you say. C'mon Kid; enjoy yourself." Dan said in retaliation.

They each took a seat around the table as the woman bartender brought over two pitchers of beer and six steins to drink it from.

"You spared no expense, did you Dan? A limousine, a bar and grill out of state, a private room to hold a party in and beer steins instead of mugs to drink out of. Does Internal Affairs know about these extracurricular activities that you've got going on, cause obviously, I don't."

"Well, Kid, I have a confession to make. The limo; we all chipped in on. Jackie's my sister so all this was free. But *you* have to pay for the drinks."

"Well then, you all better be drinking soda or water."

They all laughed.

Jackie, the bartender and owner, leaned down against her ear and whispered, "Don't let this big blowhard fool ya hon; your drinks are on the house, no matter what it is you want." She stood erect again and said aloud.

"The beers on the house, but if you want any hard liquor the restuvya will have to pay. I gotta make somethin' off this party."

"No problem sis, we understand. I already told the guys. Do you think we could get a few menus so we can eat? We're starvin'! The kid here made us work up quite an appetite just to get her here." Dan said, patting Samantha on the shoulder as they took a seat.

"Yeah sure. 'cept for the birthday girl here, you have to pay for your dinner as well."

"No problem sis."

* * *

By eight o'clock the bar was a lot busier; Samantha and the guys had eaten and drank more than their fill of beer. All but Samantha was drunk and she had three margaritas along with her share of beer.

She looked at Dan and said "I gotta go to the lady's room, could you order me a screwdriver from the bar?"

"Yeah, don't fall in." He joked.

As she opened the partition, she noticed a man step into the bar wearing a long black trench coat. With a look of desperation painted across his face, he stepped up to the bar with his right hand inside his coat. Knowing that this didn't look good, Samantha unclipped the safety snap to her holster and put her hand on the butt of it as she stepped into the small hallway leading to the restrooms.

The stranger had not seen her yet but she made sure that she was out of sight before he did. Something about him made her feel uneasy and she wished that she had brought her cell phone inside so she could call the local authorities. Dan, however, had insisted that all cell phones stay out in the limo.

Stepping into the restroom, but making sure not to close the door all the way; she waited, listened, and watched to see what was going to happen next. She couldn't see much from her view point of the bar but she *could* see the stranger pretty clear. Also, she could hear enough to form a mental picture of what she couldn't see.

From the direction of the bar, she could hear Dan calling for his sister to come over to him to order the drink that she had requested he order for her while she was gone. Immediately the stranger spoke up.

"Hey buddy, wait your turn."

"Take it easy pal; this'll just take a minute." Dan said in rebuttal.

"No, I will not wait a minute!" The man shouted as he pulled from his coat a sawed-off pump action shotgun.

"I will not wait! I'm tired of waiting!" He shouted as he pumped the gun one time and fired knocking Dan backward from his stool.

Pulling her sidearm from her holster and holding it to her side, she pushed against the door, opening it, and quickly got low to the ground to keep out of the madman's line of fire. She heard several more shots emanating from the shotgun in the direction of the back of the room and then again to the direction behind the bar.

By the time she had come out of the small hallway and to the other end of the bar opposite the man with the shotgun, he had managed to gun down the bartender, her assistant, the remaining patrons in the main room of the bar and then she heard the partition open as Clayton, McKinney, Payne, and Billie Goat came out to see what the commotion was; only to be shot down where they stood.

Seeing her fallen partner sprawled out on the barroom floor and blood quickly congregating into a large puddle beneath him, she made her way over to him only to see that his eyes were still staring widely and blindly into hers.

"Oh Dan, I'm so sorry." She whispered to him as she saw the man with the shotgun rounding the bar to the backside where the bartender and her assistant lay dead. She could only guess that he intended to rob the cash register.

Kissing her fallen partner on the forehead, she stood quickly with her police issued Glock 9mm thrust out in front of her, aiming dead on to the very monster that had taken the life of probably the best friend she had ever had in her entire life.

"I'll say this only once…" She said, looking in his direction. "Drop it!"

The stranger wheeled around on his heel and brought his shotgun up to fire, but as he did, one shot from Samantha's side arm knocked him to the floor with a single bullet between the eyes.

Running around the bar to where the monster fell to make sure that her aim was accurate and the assailant was truly dead, she arrived in time to see a thin line of blood slowly trickle out of the bullet hole in the man's forehead and a pool of blood beginning to encircle his head.

Standing behind the bar over the man she could feel hot tears begin to make their way down her face. When she looked up, she caught her reflection in the mirror and saw something strange standing toward the back of the bar. A black man dressed in a similar black overcoat that the assailant had been wearing, and a black brimmed hat covering long braided dreadlocks hanging over his shoulders stood quietly in the shadows. When she turned around to confront the stranger, she found that she was the only one left alive in the entire bar.

CHAPTER 5

Arriving at the home of Stephanie Kramer, his girlfriend, around seven thirty, Alex Rodgers had every intension of taking her out on a nice romantic date starting with a nice dinner and maybe ending with a little stroll along the beach. However, when he pulled his '67 Ford Mustang to the curb in front of her house, he found something he didn't expect.

A newer model Chevrolet Camero sat in the driveway and at first, he thought that maybe Bridget Somers, his girlfriend's roommate, might have someone over but when he looked away from the car and up at the front door, he noticed that the door was standing wide open and every light in the main part of the house was off.

Worried, he approached the front door cautiously, listening to any kind of noise coming from inside the house. Unfortunately, he heard nothing.

Stepping through the threshold and into the darkness of the living room he noticed that only one light was on in the entire house radiating from the hallway. As he neared the hallway, he could hear two voices coming from the direction of Bridget's room.

Being that he could not hear either Stephanie or Bridget's voice, he decided to find out for himself what was going on. Desperately clinging to the wall, he inched his way along the wall praying that neither girl was home and that the men he was hearing were simply there to rob the place.

As he neared Bridget's door, he listened to the men standing inside as they talked to one another. Trying to discern what they were up to, Alex heard something that made his skin crawl.

"I want the bitch first." One guy said.

"No way, I'm first." The other one said.

"Screw you dude, I'm going first." The first said again.

Noticing that the door had been left open a crack and that it opened in to the left, Alex quickly crossed to the other side so he could get a better look. When he peered through the gap, he saw what he had feared he would see. Inside, Bridget lay screaming silently through taped lips as tears flowed from her blindfolded eyes. She still had her clothes on but one man held in his grip, a pocket knife in which Alex was sure was going to be used to rid her of that problem.

Her sheets had been ripped into separate pieces in order to tie Bridget to her bed from one post to the next and both men stood over her as they argued. Alex could only imagine the horror in which Bridget was enduring at that very moment, hearing them as they talked about what they wanted to do to her.

Both men looked to be in their late teens to early twenties and wore similar colors of clothing which told Alex that they might be members of some kind of local gang but since gangs wasn't really his area of expertise, he wasn't for sure. Their intensions, however, were evidently crystal clear on what they were going to do.

As the rage began to build within him, giving him strength and courage to do what he knew needed to be done, Alex burst into the room and grabbed the closest man to the door from behind and snapped his neck with one quick twist of his hands. The second man turned in reaction, raising a pistol in his right hand to the sudden intrusion but before he could act, Alex pulled the knife from the fallen man's grip and threw it over handed at the man holding the gun, hitting him dead center in the throat.

Before the pistol could even fire, the second man dropped dead to the floor. Retrieving the dead man's gun from the floor and placing it in the waistband of his pants, Alex quickly moved over to Bridget and freed her of her restraints even as she continued to scream through her duct tape. When he removed her blindfold and she could see who it was rescuing her, her screaming stopped and her tears became that of joy and relief.

With her hands now free, Bridget wrapped her arms around his neck and pulled him close to her, squeezing with every ounce of strength she could muster in gratitude.

"Where's Steph?" He asked when she finally released him from her grip.

"I think she's in the other room with the other one." She said as a strained and worried look came over her face.

"Do you know how many there are?"

"I only saw three when they came in."

"Okay, go next door and call the police, but don't come back inside." Alex said as he helped her to her feet and checked the hallway to ensure that no one was coming to investigate any noise that may have erupted from his scuffle with the two men merely seconds ago.

Seeing that the coast was clear, he ushered her into the hallway and waited until she was safely out of the light and most likely on her way next door before proceeding further down the hall to the only other bedroom in the house; Stephanie's.

The door was completely shut so there was no way of slipping into the room unnoticed, but he did see a bit of good luck, the light in her room was on. There was no way that anyone inside would see a shadow approaching from under the door, being that the hallway light was on as well. Sneaking up close to the door to listen to whatever he could from within the room, he waited for the right moment to act.

"I'm going to give you somethin' I bet you've never had before." A man said with a deep and rough voice.

Fearing that the worst was about to happen to the love of his life, Alex burst through the door and saw a large black man straddling his girlfriend's waist. He was in the process of sliding down between her legs as if he were a snake coiling up before it struck when Alex opened the door.

"What the fu…" The man said, looking up at Alex with surprise on his face. Reaching behind his back to a pistol tucked deep in the waistband of his pants, he gripped the handle and slid it smoothly out and aimed it at Alex's face.

Unfortunately for this stranger, however, Alex was too quick for him as he moved away from the door and quickly toward his girlfriend's assailant, grabbing him by the seat of his pants with one hand and the back of his shirt with the other and pulled.

The man was yanked off of Stephanie and hauled to the floor where he crashed hard. When he started to get to his feet, he grabbed hold of the pistol once again and took aim at Alex. Alex reacted quickly to the gun and with one kick to the man's outstretched wrist, sent the gun flying away from his grip.

"What the fuck man?" The man said.

"You picked the wrong house." Alex said as he allowed the stranger to get to his feet.

"Go ahead, get your piece." Alex said, letting him go for the gun.

Instead of reaching for the gun, the stranger took a swing at him but Alex was quicker. With one fluid motion, Alex pulled the pistol that he had removed from one of the other assailants in the other room and pulled the trigger, repainting the wall behind the man a crimson red.

Releasing Stephanie of her bonds, Alex helped her to her feet and took her blindfold off of her face. "Alex?" She said surprised to see him and then threw her arms around him and squeezed hard nearly choking him to death.

"C'mon, let's get outta here." He said, helping her to her feet and walking her out of the room.

* * *

With Stephanie safely outside on a porch swing that hung just to the right of the front door, Alex told her that he needed to leave.

"Why?" She said looking into his eyes.

"Because of what I did in there."

"You saved our lives." Stephanie said.

"Yes, but I killed all three of those men to do it and I don't think the police are going to look too highly on me for that."

"But where are you gonna go?"

"I'm just going to drive around for about ten minutes or so and then pull back up here as if I was just gettin' here. That way, they'll never know otherwise." He explained.

"I don't understand why you have to go. I'm sure if you tell them that what you did was to save us; they'd understand." Stephanie said still objecting.

From next door, Bridget appeared running across the lawn to meet them. "Stephanie… oh, I'm so glad you're okay." She said as she collapsed into the swing and wrapped her arms around her long-time friend.

Fearing that he was quickly running out of time, Alex explained to both girls what he wanted them to say to the police when they arrived leaving out any involvement from him. "If the police ask who saved your lives or who killed those men inside, tell them you didn't recognize who it was but are very grateful that they arrived when they did. If they ask if you can describe the person, tell them that everything happened so fast that you can't remember." Alex concluded.

"Alex… I don't like having to lie to the police." Stephanie said.

"If you don't, they could put me away for life."

"But Alex…"

"Steph, please… just tell them what I told you to tell them. Okay?"

"I'll tell them." Bridget said.

"You just stay quiet as though you're in shock. They'll leave you alone as long as they think you can't talk to them." She said, looking now at Stephanie.

Stephanie nodded in agreement and Alex quickly kissed her on the lips and then ran across the yard to his car, got in, and drove away. Within only a few minutes after seeing his taillights fade away out of sight, the sounds of police sirens rose in the distance.

* * *

Going inside to the coat closet in the living room, Bridget pulled down a blanket that they normally used when curling up on either the couch or the recliner when watching movies, and went back outside and covered both she and Stephanie in the blanket.

The neighbors in whom Bridget had interrupted their night in order to use their telephone, Charlie and Mary Atkins, came over from next door to see if they could be of some comfort to either of the girls just as the first patrol cars pulled up to the curb in front of the house.

From behind the wheel of the cruiser stepped a rookie officer whom none of them knew, followed by a very familiar face to both of them; Sergeant Alan Perkins.

Alan had been a good friend of Alex and Stephanie's, but Bridget always thought of him as a jerk. It made her exceptionally happy to think that she would be the one answering all of the questions she was sure he was bound to ask. With what seemed like legitimate concern, he approached them and asked them each if they were okay.

"Yes, Alan, we're fine. But I wouldn't say the same for the assholes that attacked us. They're inside." Bridget said sarcastically, motioning like a hitchhiker thumbing a ride for him to look inside.

"I'll be right back to talk to you two." Alan said.

"Looking forward to it." Bridget smarted off as she turned to Stephanie and said, "Why is my life filled with assholes tonight?"

Stephanie made a slight grin and whispered, "Thank God for Alex."

Bridget returned her grin and hugged her.

Within minutes after the first cruiser arrived, four others joined them as well as an unmarked Ford sedan in which a plain clothes detective stepped out from behind the driver's seat and approached them wearing a tattered brown trench coat as though he were trying to mimic some TV detective.

"Who are you supposed to be?" Bridget smarted off when the man stepped onto the porch.

"My name's Detective Marshall O'Grady." The man said as other officers began entering the house. "Do you mind if I ask you ladies a few questions?"

"Sure Detective, what do you need to know?" Bridget said.

Opening a notepad and taking out a pen as though he were a Pulitzer Prize winning reporter O'Grady said, "Can either of you tell me what happened here?"

"We were attacked; that's what." Bridget said.

"Can you identify your attackers?" O'Grady asked as he began writing down something in the notepad.

Before Bridget could say anything else, Alan appeared at the doorway and said, "Detective... I think you're gonna want to see this."

"I'll be right back ladies." O'Grady said, putting both the pen and notepad into an inside liner pocket of his coat and followed Alan into the house.

Minutes later, he returned saying, "Can either of you tell me what happened to those three men inside?"

"Not really Detective. All I know is that one minute those goons are trying to do God awful things to us and the next thing I know is... they're dead. We both had blindfolds on so when we took them off, whoever it was that saved us was gone." Bridget said, realizing that this story might actually save them more grief than trying Alex's concocted story.

"Miss Kramer; would you agree with that statement?" O'Grady asked Stephanie who played up her role of being in a state of shock.

Saying nothing, she put her head on Bridget's shoulder and Bridget answered for her by saying, "Look Detective… we've both had a hell of a night and if you don't mind, we'd love it if you got that garbage out of our house so we can just get some sleep."

"Okay Miss Somers… but I don't think you're going to be able to sleep in this house for a little while longer. Right now, it's a crime scene and until our guys can wrap up this case, you're going to have to stay in a hotel or something." O'Grady said just as an ambulance pulled up to the curb.

"Better yet… Larkin! Take these two in the ambulance to the hospital and get them looked at." O'Grady said, hollering to one of the uniformed officers taking statements from the Atkins'.

"Yes sir." Officer Brian Larkin said as the paramedics arrived to escort both Stephanie and Bridget to the ambulance to be taken to the hospital.

"I still need to speak with you both some more Miss Somers, I might be along a little bit later to ask you some more question. If you don't mind that is." O'Grady said as he watched them being escorted by the paramedics to the back of the ambulance.

"Looking forward to it Detective." Bridget said. "Do you think you can do me a favor though since you're gong to make a trip over to the hospital anyway…?"

"If I can."

"If you get time while you're inside looking around; do you think you could get us some clean clothes? After what just happened, we kinda feel a little dirty."

"I'll get you some right now." Alan said as he turned to go back inside the house.

"Thank you, Detective."

Once Stephanie and Bridget were both inside the ambulance, Alan rushed outside with a bundle of clothes in his hands to the patrol car in which Brian was using to follow the ambulance to the hospital.

"Take these clothes with you and make sure they know that I did my best to find something for them to wear." Alan said, placing the clothes in the front seat of Brian's car.

"Sure, thing Alan." Brian said.

Turning to go back inside the house, Detective O'Grady was followed soon thereafter by Alan who took only one more look in the direction of Bridget and Stephanie before disappearing inside the house.

* * *

Looking down at the two men sprawled on the floor of the first bedroom they came to, Detective O'Grady and Alan began carefully looking through their pockets for identification but came up empty.

"Now why would these guys wanna come in here and try to rape these lovely young ladies?" Detective O'Grady said in his deep southern drawl.

"Were they just here to rob them but when they found them home, decided to have a little fun?" O'Grady continued. "Has anyone touched anything?"

"No sir."

"Good, get everyone else outta here until the crime lab boys have a crack at this place." O'Grady said.

"Yes sir." Alan said as he rounded up the other officers to have them all go outside to question neighbors and collect whatever evidence they could outside.

Leaving the first bedroom shortly after he heard Alan outside, O'Grady stepped into the second bedroom that lay at the end of the hall. There, he found the third slain assailant with his head resting against the wall with a bullet between his eyes and his body slumped onto the floor.

Pulling the latex gloves from his hands as he stepped out onto the porch, he noticed a car pull up to the curb, parking where the ambulance had just minutes ago and a young man step out of the car.

Upon noticing the man, O'Grady watched as Alan quickly made his way over to the man, stopping him before he even had a chance to round the car. A couple of seconds later, the man got back behind the steering wheel and took off in the direction that the ambulance had gone moments ago.

"What was that all about Sergeant?" O'Grady said as Alan made his way back up to the porch.

"That was one of the victim's boyfriends. His name's Alex Rodgers. He said he was coming by to take her out to dinner and wanted to know what was going on."

"Which girl?"

"Stephanie Kramer."

"Ahh… the silent one. What did you tell him?"

"Only that there was a domestic disturbance, that she had been injured and was in route to the hospital for observation, and that she needed to see you as soon as she was done at the hospital."

"So, he was just getting here then?"

"From what I could tell."

"See what you can find out from the neighbors, maybe someone saw something, I'm gonna have a talk with our two victims."

"Already taken care of sir. I'll have the reports sent to me over the radio. I'll go with you. I'd like to find out what happened as well. Both girls are pretty good friends of mine."

"If you wish… get in; I planned to take your car anyway."

* * *

Alex made it to the hospital emergency room ten minutes after the ambulance had arrived. A police officer was sitting in the waiting room as he walked in. He knew him too; Brian Larkin.

Brian was a puny man for a police officer, so scrawny that his clothes seemed to hang off of him. He could never find adult clothes that would fit him right and police uniforms didn't always come in the size that he could easily fit into. His waist was so thin that his belt – the smallest the department had to issue – wrapped around him almost twice just to keep his pants above his waist.

When Alex walked into the ER waiting room, Brian stood tall most likely thinking that Alex was one of his superiors coming to check on him. But when he noticed who it really was, he allowed himself to loosen up and came over to Alex to shake his hand.

"Alex… I didn't expect you to get here so quick." Brian said, extending his hand.

Careful not to tip his hand in this crooked game of living poker, Alex acted as if he knew nothing of what had happened and approached Brian with as much ignorance of the situation that he could pretend. "What's going on Brian? I heard something happened and that Stephanie was brought here."

"Actually Alex… they're both here." Brian said.

"How are they? Are either of them hurt?" Alex said, keeping up his pretense of not knowing what was really going on.

"Don't know; we've only been here for about ten minutes. I'm not even sure if they've been seen by a doctor yet." Brian said.

"I'm going to go back and see them." Alex said, patting Brian on the shoulder as he went by him.

Making it look good because he knew that Brian had followed him into the ER, Alex asked Stephanie when he saw her, "Are you alright? What happened?"

Seeing that Brian was right behind him, Stephanie kept up the charade that she was in total shock when she saw Alex but then broke down and started crying as she nearly leaped from the table into his arms.

"It's okay." Brian said, trying to comfort her from behind Alex, "It's all over now."

"Thank you, Brian." Alex answered for his girlfriend. "Would you mind giving us a little privacy?"

"Sure… I'll be right out in the waiting room if you need anything." Brian said, taking a couple of steps back toward the waiting area and then turned to exit the door leading out of the ER.

* * *

Detective O'Grady walked through the emergency room doors leading into the waiting room nearly half an hour after Alex had arrived. Brian stood straight as an arrow when he saw the detective walk through the door.

"Officer Larkin… has Alex Rodgers arrived here yet?" O'Grady asked stepping over to him.

"Yes sir… he's in with his girlfriend and Miss Somers now."

"You let him go in to see them and didn't stay in there with him?"

"Sir? You didn't tell me I needed to watch Alex." Brian said with a look of confusion on his face.

Alan stepped up behind the detective and said, "Why would he need to watch Alex, Detective O'Grady? Is he suspected of doing something wrong?"

Deciding not to answer either man, O'Grady pivoted on one foot and walked through the door into the ER area to find both Alex Rodgers and the two girls. When he spotted the girls in a little corner of the room surrounded only by a curtained wall, he walked up to Alex and grabbed him by his right arm, pulling him close to him so that only Alex could hear what he had to say.

"Mr. Rodgers, may I speak with you a moment?" O'Grady said.

"Do I know you?" Alex asked, turning to the detective who still had hold of his arm.

Letting go of Alex's arm he said, "I'm sorry… where are my manners? My name is Detective Marshall O'Grady; I'm new to the precinct and handling this investigation."

"What investigation? I'm still in the dark here of what actually happened." Alex said.

"Sir, I don't wish to upset the ladies anymore than they already are. If you would kindly step with me out into the waiting room so that we may talk privately, I would appreciate it." O'Grady said.

"Of course," Alex said, kissing Stephanie and telling her that he would be right back.

With Brian offering to stay behind and look after the girls in his stead, Alex walked through the doors leading back into the waiting room with Detective O'Grady and Alan following close behind.

"What's this all about?" Asked Alex as the door shut behind Alan.

"Well Mr. Rodgers, let's start out by telling me how much you know right now." O'Grady said.

"Only what Alan… I mean Sgt. Perkins… has told me. That there was some kind of domestic dispute at my girlfriend's house and that one or both of the girls had been injured and were sent here." Alex said, trying to play out his role of ignorance to the best of his ability.

"Neither of the girls have spoken to you about what happened?"

"No, you two arrived shortly before I could even get my girlfriend to say anything other than my name. Whatever happened… it sure rattled her cage."

"What about Miss Somers? Did she tell you anything that happened?"

"Bridget? No, she's been trying to console Stephanie. The only thing she said to me was that Stephanie hasn't said a word since the ordeal and she's been trying to get her to say something – anything. Do you want to tell me what's going on?"

"Have a seat Mr. Rodgers…"

"Please… call me Alex."

"Okay… Alex… what I'm about to tell you might trigger some emotions and I would rather you be sitting before I say anything." O'Grady said.

"Okay." Alex said, taking a seat in the comforts provided by the hospital.

"Tonight… someone had broken into Miss Kramer and Miss Somers's home. We're uncertain, as of yet, whether they knew the girls were home when they entered or not but there *are* signs that a struggle had ensued and both girls were taken into their respective bedrooms. From the evidence we gathered at the scene, they may have been raped and most assuredly murdered had someone not intervened."

"Raped? Did you just say raped?" Alex said playing the role to the hilt.

"Please, Mr. Rodgers… Alex… calm down. Let me finish."

Alex crossed his arms and sat back in the seat trying to maintain an angry but 'willing to cooperate' composure as O'Grady continued.

"Apparently, their plans were foiled by an unknown fourth person. We're unsure if there were originally four men involved in the break-in and one of them turned on the other three or if some completely different person came into the picture and interrupted them."

"You did get them… right? I mean… the bastards are behind bars… aren't they?" Alex said, trying to keep his words calm.

"Well, that's what I'm trying to get at… someone interrupted them and now… they're all dead. All except this mysterious fourth person."

"Well, how do you know there were only four? Maybe there were more than that."

"No, I'm pretty sure that there were only four other people in that house besides the girls. The car outside is registered to one of the assailants and it's only big enough to maybe fit four at the most." O'Grady said.

"Maybe there was another vehicle there." Alex argued.

"Maybe; but I doubt it belonged to the three inside or anyone associated with them either." O'Grady said. "Which brings me to the question I have for you Mr. Rodgers… where were you before arriving at the house conveniently at the time in which you did?"

"*Conveniently*? What are you trying to get at Detective?" Alex said as he began to get irate at the implication that O'Grady was trying to get him to admit to. True as it might be, he wasn't about to tell them they were correct.

"Mr. Rodgers… calm down. There's no need for you to get angry at me. If you think about it, I'm sure you can see my view of this."

"I'm listening."

"Being that you *are* the boyfriend to one of the victims; it would only fit the theory that you walked in on these three intruders, maybe caught them in the act of doing something unspeakable to one or both girls, and you reacted with savage revenge. The next thing you know, three men are dead and you're standing there with blood on your hands." O'Grady said, nailing it almost exactly as it had happened.

With a look of total shock on his face, but not letting on the real reason behind it, Alex said, "What the hell are you smoking? That theory sounds good and all if I *had* arrived sooner than I did. Don't think for one second that if I had I wouldn't have done everything you just said but unfortunately, for me – for you, that's just not the way it is."

"Well Mr. Rodgers, we have to look at all angles. We can't really rule anything out." O'Grady said.

Disgusted with the implications that O'Grady was throwing at him, Alex got to his feet and began making his way back to the ER area to be with Stephanie and Bridget when O'Grady stood and blocked his way.

"Something else you need to say to me Detective?" Alex said as his calmness was starting to wear paper thin.

"You seem awfully angry Mr. Rodgers; almost defensive even. Might I ask why that is?" O'Grady said.

"Oh, I don't know, maybe because some asshole is accusing me of something I had nothing to do with!" Alex said as he stepped up into O'Grady's face.

Alan quickly intervened and shoved his way in between the two, turning to face Alex as he did so in order to push him to back up a little.

"You seem really hostile now Mr. Rodgers… you also seem to have a problem with people of authority. Would I be correct in that assumption?" O'Grady pressed.

"Alex… Don't let him get you riled up." Alan said, but was afraid his words were falling on deaf ears as Alex retaliated.

"Not at all Detective… at least not to those who are actually *in* authority over me. Last time I checked Detective, you weren't one of them."

"Okay, let me rephrase the question."

"Don't bother, I know what you meant. I have a problem with assholes putting their hands on my girlfriend and me not able to do anything about it. I have an even bigger problem with assholes making accusations about me without any evidence to back it up!" Alex said as his voice began to rise in octave as his anger began to boil over.

"Maybe we should discuss this later." Alan intersected.

"Maybe you're right Sergeant… I believe Mr. Rodgers here has some thinking to do." O'Grady said.

"Oh, you can discuss whatever you want all you want whenever you want. Just leave me out of it!" Alex said boiling over. "Now if you'll excuse me; I have a girlfriend that needs my attention a whole lot more than you do right now." Alex said sarcastically.

* * *

By ten o'clock, the hospital finally released both girls. The police had finally left and Alex was sure both girls needed some rest. Going outside to his car, he brought it around to the entrance/exit of the emergency room and parked. Leaving the engine idling, he got out and was on his way back inside when someone grabbed him by the arm.

Detective O'Grady stood behind him with one hand on Alex's arm, which he released when Alex turned to face him. "Now what do you want?" Alex asked sarcastically.

"I think maybe we started off on the wrong foot Mr. Rodgers. I would like to see both you and the girls in my office at your earliest convenience tomorrow morning. I have some questions for both ladies and I might have a few more for you as well." O'Grady said.

"I don't have anything else to tell you Detective except… if you ever put your hands on me again, it better be to arrest me for something or I'll file a harassment charge on you and maybe even an assault charge if it suits me." Alex said as he walked angrily away from O'Grady and into the hospital to gather both Stephanie and Bridget to take to his house for the night.

* * *

"I don't understand this Rodgers guy." O'Grady said to Sgt. Alan Perkins when he got back into the passenger seat of Alan's car. "Is he normally like this toward law enforcement officers?"

"Pretty much… to those he doesn't know anyway. Good guy though, give you the shirt right off his back whether he knew you or not." Alan said, putting the car in gear.

"What does he have against law enforcement?"

"Well sir, it's like this… When Alex was about fifteen; his older brother, Garry, died in a convenience store robbery gone completely wrong. He was shopping late one night and the place was robbed while he was still inside. The burglars were nervous or scared or both and ended up shooting everyone inside the store because *they* thought they couldn't get caught if there were no witnesses. Unfortunately for them, everyone that they shot lived through the ordeal except for Garry.

"Garry had been shot in the chest. The gunmen had fired so wildly that they didn't have a clue if they hit anything or not until they saw that everyone was down. They ran out of the store and were caught nearly three blocks down. However, the two officers that had investigated the case were on the take. The two kids were part of a local gang and had robbed the store as part of the gang's initiation. The gang leaders paid off the two cops and the cops in turn ended up pinning the robbery and all of the assaults somehow on Alex's brother. It was bad cops like that that drove Larkin and I to join the force; to change the image of law enforcement in our city. Alex, however, respects the badge until it gets in his face."

"Well, that would explain his hostility a little." O'Grady admitted. "But why would he have a problem with me? I wasn't even here when that stuff went down with his brother."

"He is somewhat over the past; but he doesn't know you. You shouldn't take it personally. He tends to be a little cynical at times."

"Well, let's go find out what the crime lab came up with. I still have a lot of questions that I need to ask Miss Kramer and Miss Somers if we're going to get to the bottom of this case. I'll try to avoid asking him questions but I can't guarantee anything." O'Grady said.

"As long as you're fair Detective in how you deal with him, he'll be respectful."

"Well, if the crime lab comes back with what I think they will… he might not like me once I start asking questions to him again and this time, he might have a good reason." O'Grady said.

* * *

By ten thirty, Alex pulled into the driveway in front of his house. He got out of the car and opened the door for both Stephanie and Bridget to get out. He then went to the front door and after unlocking it, stood to one side to allow them to enter first.

When he stepped through the doorway, the phone began ringing. Picking up the receiver Alex said, "Hello."

"Is this Alex Rodgers?" A voice said on the other end.

"Yes, it is. Who's this?"

"Sorry to be calling so late Mr. Rodgers but this is quite important."

"That's okay, I suppose; who is this?"

"I'm sorry, my name is Clayton Green. I'm an attorney in Augusta, Maine. I represent…"

"I'm sorry, did you just say Maine; as in the state of Maine?"

"Yes sir, I represent the late Shane Stevenson. Does that name sound familiar?"

"No, should it?"

"Well, it seems after careful investigation we've found that you are one of Mr. Stevenson's grandchildren."

"I'm sorry, I don't understand. I don't know any Shane Stevenson. You must have the wrong number." Alex said, beginning to hang up the phone when he heard the man on the other end of the line ask a question that stopped him short.

"Were you adopted as a child Mr. Rodgers?"

"What did you just say?" Alex said, pulling the receiver back up to his ear.

"Were you adopted as a child Mr. Rodgers?"

"Yes, I was. How did you know that?" Alex said.

"As I said, Mr. Rodgers, my company has been doing some extensive investigating. You were adopted by a Michael and Kathleen Rodgers twenty-one years ago. Your mother, your biological mother, was Sabrina Elliot, Shane Stevenson's daughter. Her husband, your biological father, was Robert Elliot; a fisherman along the coast of Maine..."

"Okay, you have my attention," Alex interrupted. "How the hell did you find all this out? Adoption records are sealed; it would take an act of Congress to get into them."

"That and money hungry friends in high places. Look Mr. Rodgers, your grandfather was a very wealthy man in his own right. He has left everything that he owned and the money your father had willed to you to his only surviving relatives; you and… your sister."

"My what?" Alex said surprised.

"Your older sister, Samantha, was also adopted. She, however, was old enough to have a choice on whether she wanted to keep her last name or change it. Her adopted parents respected her wishes when she decided that she to keep it. Your grandfather has left an equal amount of money for the two of you as well as a house and property. I will need you here in Augusta by the end of this month to sign papers if you wish to accept your part of this will, Mr. Rodgers."

"The end of the month, that's less than a week away. I can't afford to fly up there."

"A ticket has already been purchased for you and a guest; it's waiting for you at the airport. A password is needed in order for you to pick it up. Use the code word *'Brunswick'* to pick it up. Once you land in the Bangor International Airport you will have to travel by car south along Interstate

95 about 2 hours here to Augusta." Green said as he continued to give the remaining directions.

"Why in the world are we traveling all the way to Bangor if you're in Augusta?"

"I'm sorry to say that there isn't an airport big enough here in Augusta for the type of plane that you'll be traveling on. The two nearest airports would be Bangor or South Portland's Jetport. Believe it or not, the trip to Bangor will be a little cheaper than the trip to South Portland and Augusta is pretty much dead center of the two in distance."

"Brunswick…" Alex pondered. "Why the name Brunswick?"

"That's the name of the house, Mr. Rodgers. The Brunswick House."

Captain Timothy Ford arrived at the Kansas City Police Department shortly before three in the morning. After receiving a call from their Captain nearly four and half hours earlier informing him of the horrific incident that had taken place at one of their local bars involving his detectives, he hurriedly got out of bed and began making his way to the interstate.

Six of his homicide detectives were involved in the massacre but only one survived; the birthday girl. Walking up to the dispatcher's window he said, "I'm here to pick up Detective Samantha Elliot."

A chubby dark-haired woman sitting behind the desk wearing a headset looked up at him and said, "Sure, you must be her Captain. She's been waiting for you to get here; she's pretty shaken up."

The woman unhooked her headset from a little box attached to the phone system and walked to the back.

"Could I speak with your Captain as well?" Ford hollered out as the woman disappeared.

Minutes later, Samantha walked through a door to his left followed by another, much older, woman. "Are you okay Sam?" Ford said truly concerned for her and by her pale look.

"I'll be fine, I'm gonna wait in the car if that's alright." She said wearily.

"Yeah, go ahead. I need to speak with the captain for a minute. I'll be out there shortly." He said, opening the door for her.

"I'm Captain Victoria Seely; you must be Captain Ford." The woman said, extending her hand in a friendly greeting.

"Yes…" Ford said, taking the woman's hand. "Can I be blunt Captain?"

"I suppose."

"What the hell happened?"

"My best guess is a robbery gone totally wrong. Detective Elliot says she saw the man enter the bar and admitted that he looked a little suspicious. She told me she kept an eye on him until she saw her partner approach the bar and then she went into the lady's room.

"When the shooting started, she told me she pulled her sidearm and cautiously approached from the lady's room where she found her fallen partner and the assailant standing over several other dead patrons with a shotgun. Miraculously, she took the assailant out without being shot herself and then phoned 9-1-1 from the bar phone. She's pretty broken up about this guy named Dan; I'm guessing was her partner. She's been nearly catatonic since we arrived. It took us about an hour to get anything out of her." Captain Seely stated.

"Dan Riley *was* her partner and best friend – kind of like a father figure you could say. He orchestrated this little party for her because it was her birthday."

"Some birthday… Poor kid, I feel for her."

"Yeah, I hope she'll be alright. I'd appreciate a call when you're finished with my men so that I can give them a proper burial."

"Sure. It should be only a day or two."

* * *

They drove for nearly an hour before either of them said anything to the other. Finally, Captain Ford could take the silence no longer.

"Samantha, I'm talking to you as both your Captain and as Tim, your friend. You're going to snap out of this. You got the bastard that killed Dan and the others. He's not going to be doing this again. You did it. You stopped him. Dan, Bruce, Robert, Jack, Bill; they're not going to think anything different of you just because you didn't get out of the restroom a minute sooner or later. You did all you could and most importantly, you didn't get dead doing it. When we get back, I want you to take some time off. I want you to talk to the police psychiatrist and when you're ready to come back; we'll all be waiting for you." Captain Ford said.

"Why did this have to happen?"

"I wish I could answer that Sam. I truly do."

Looking out the passenger side window, away from him, she said, "I just don't know what else to say. I can remember my parents being killed twenty-one years ago; I mean I was only five, but I can still remember it. My brother was six months old, still so tiny. I remember we were in a bank getting money for something when these men rushed in wearing masks and firing their guns in the air like wild men.

"I remember my dad catching my brother in midair as my mother fell motionless to the floor when one of those bastards shot her. Dad covered us both with his own body as they began to shoot up the place. It wasn't a robbery; it was a massacre just like at the bar."

"That's terrible. Why haven't you talked about this sooner?"

Ignoring the question and continuing with her story she said, "A police officer rolled my father off of us and, after prying my brother from his death grip, helped me to my feet. He held my face against his leg so that I couldn't see that everyone in the bank was dead; but I knew. My father had saved our lives by sacrificing his own. A plain clothes woman detective, who I found out later was here on vacation from Texas, had shot and killed the man that killed my parents and took us back to the station where Child Welfare picked us up. A few days later, we were presented to our only living relative, my grandfather. He took us in for about six months until he had a stroke. Child Welfare stepped in again and they put us in foster care.

"Within a month, my brother was adopted. I was adopted nine and a half months later. You know, up until now, I hadn't even thought about my brother, or that day, in a long time."

"Have you ever tried to track your brother down?"

"No, hadn't thought about it. Hell, I haven't seen him since he was adopted. I wouldn't even know where to begin."

"Well, take the time Sam. You're a detective for God's sake; track him down, get a little family reunion together, and go from there. You'll be fine, you'll see."

* * *

At eight o'clock, Captain Ford pulled into Samantha's apartment complex parking area. Samantha was passed out in the passenger seat.

After all that she had been through, he knew she needed to rest but woke her anyway.

"Do you need me to walk you up?" He asked when he was sure she was awake.

"No, I'll be fine. I'm probably just going to crash."

"Okay, call me if you need me, day or night." Ford said as she got out of the car.

* * *

The rain fell hard against the ground. So hard, that it bounced four inches as it splashed against it. The thunder cracked against the night sky and the lightning illuminated it, giving the night flashes of bright light.

The shutters on the second-floor windows banged against the window frames from the tremendous force of the wind. The front door of the house seemed to be standing wide open this time and inside lay a huge foyer where women's clothing lay ripped and torn on the floor just inside the door.

At the stairway, not more than twenty-five to fifty feet inside and to the right, she could hear some kind of commotion emanating from up the stairs. Drawing nearer to the stairwell, blood trickled slowly down the stairs as if it were water dripping from a spigot.

At the top of the staircase now lay a dark figure; it seemed to be the source of the blood. As the silhouette began to become more and more in focus, a loud buzzing sound brought Samantha quickly out of her nightmare and back into reality.

Rising from her bed in a cold sweat and a quick gasp, as if she had been holding her breath, she breathed hard and deep until she felt that her lungs were amply filled and a sigh of relief escaped her lips. It had only been a dream.

She had made it up to her apartment and hit the bed in such a fugue state that she barely remembered even doing it. From the bed stand beside her bed, she could see the light blinking on her answering machine. She had been so exhausted when she got home that she'd forgotten to check her messages.

Glancing over to her machine, she found a single digit illuminated on the digital readout. She had only one message. She looked at her caller ID to see where the call had originated but didn't recognize the number. However, the alpha message told her that the call had originated in Augusta, Maine.

Playing the message on the machine, she listened intently as a man's gentle voice came on the line. "Miss Elliot, my name is Clayton Green, an attorney for the late Shane Stevenson. I'm out of Augusta, Maine. If you could; please contact me here at my office. It is very important that I speak with you; day or night, please call."

When the beep came signaling the end of the message, Samantha picked up the phone which was seated beside the answering machine and dialed the number listed on the caller ID. "Law offices of Clayton Green and Associates, Melissa speaking; how may I assist you?" A female voice announced as the call was picked up.

"Yes, I need to speak with Mr. Clayton Green please."

"Can I say who's calling?"

"Samantha Elliot."

"Thank you. One moment please." The secretary said as she put Samantha on hold.

Within a minute, the man's voice that had graced her machine the night before came over the line. "Miss Elliot, I've been trying to reach you since eight o'clock last night. Is everything alright?"

"No, not really but that doesn't matter right now. You called me last night saying something about representing Shane Stevenson." Samantha said. "I haven't heard that name in quite a while. What's wrong with my grandfather?"

"Well, it's my deepest regret to inform you that your grandfather recently passed away after suffering a brain aneurysm. In his will, he has left an equal amount of money as well as a house and property to you and your brother." Green explained.

"Well, I'm sorry to tell you this, but I have no way of telling you how to contact him. I haven't seen him in quite a number of years."

"I've already contacted your brother and he should be h…"

"What did you just say?" Samantha interrupted, sitting more upright than she already was in her bed.

"Let me explain Miss Elliot. Months before your grandfather passed away, he hired my firm to draw up and handle his last will and testament. He explained that you both were his only living relatives and that you had been adopted. He also explained that he had no idea where either of you were.

"He paid a lot of money to track you both down. I contacted your brother last night and it sounds as if he'll be here by the end of the week; which is good because I need you both here by then to complete the final paperwork."

"Are you sure it was him? Where is he? Who is he? How did you…" Samantha started asking all at once.

"His name is Alex Rodgers now. He's working as a restaurant cook in Georgia."

"How is it that you were able to find him; he was adopted as a baby. Those records are sealed even to me. How is it you were able to get this information and I couldn't? I'm his sister and a cop for God's sake!"

"All I can say is that my firm has its ways of acquiring the kind of information that most people are unable to get. I'll explain more in depth when you arrive."

"How is my brother getting to Augusta?"

"By plane; there's a ticket for you and a guest as well at the Tulsa International Airport. If you use the code word '*Brunswick*' when you get there, you shouldn't have any problems picking it up. The plane will arrive at the Bangor International Airport. From there, you'll have to travel by car south to Augusta on Interstate 95."

"Bangor? Why Bangor?"

"As I told your brother, I'm sorry to say, there are no major airports here in Augusta and the closest one is either Bangor or South Portland. Bangor seems to be the obvious choice because believe it or not, it's a little cheaper. It'll take you approximately two hours to reach our office from the airport once you arrive."

"Okay, I'll be there in two days Mr. Green. Thank you," she said.

After hanging up the phone, Samantha plopped back on her bed and stared at the ceiling in both astonishment and bewilderment at the idea that she would soon be seeing her little brother again. She didn't know exactly what to think or do. But this seemed like just what the doctor ordered.

The clock from Alex's car radio showed that it was nine-thirty when they arrived at the Atlanta Police Department. The girls really weren't all that awake when Alex got them up but he was eager to get all of this questioning out of the way.

Walking up to the huge desk that stood just inside the door of the waiting room, Alex asked the desk sergeant if he could inform Detective O'Grady that they were there and then gave their names. A few minutes later, the sergeant led them back behind the wall and up one flight of stairs to an office and told them to have a seat.

"Detective O'Grady will be with you in a few minutes. There's coffee around the corner so feel free to help yourself." The sergeant said as he turned and walked back down the stairs.

"Thank you." Alex said as he took a seat and tried to get comfortable, anxious to get all the questioning out of the way; he hated police stations with a passion.

"Now, just remember, they're gonna separate us to get your statements. He's already asked me all the questions I think he's going to ask me but I'm sure he's coming up with more. Just tell him the truth the best you can; leaving my involvement out of course." Alex whispered to the girls once the desk sergeant was safely out of earshot.

"What if they search your car while we're in here?" Bridget whispered.

"Already taken care of; I always keep a change of clothes with a couple of extra shirts to be on the safe side in the trunk of my car. After I left the house last night, I changed my clothes and bundled the old clothes up, weighted them down with a rock, and threw them in the river."

"Original. What about the gun?" Stephanie whispered this time.

"Wrapped it up in the shirt as well; it's safely at the bottom of the river never to be seen again." Alex said.

* * *

Detective O'Grady walked into the office approximately fifteen minutes after they arrived. Stephanie and Bridget were taken to another office while O'Grady kept Alex in his.

"I've got some interesting information Mr. Rodgers. Our crime scene investigators have found several fingerprints throughout both rooms where this crime occurred and many of them are yours. Do you care to explain this?" O'Grady said, sitting down on the side of his desk slapping a manila folder full of papers against his thigh looking pretty proud of himself.

Grinning, Alex said, "Sure." He was all too happy to burst O'Grady's bubble. He knew during his entrance into the house that night he had not touched anything with his hands other than the intruders. He doubted that they would find any prints on the bodies.

Taking a seat in front of the desk and settling in for what would probably be a long morning Alex said, "Okay, I'll tell you what Detective; let me answer your question with one of my own."

"Why?"

"Well, if we're going to play this game, I want to be able to ask some questions too, that is unless I'm under arrest; in which case you might want to ask all these questions behind a two-way mirror."

"No – no; you're not under arrest. Go ahead, ask your question." O'Grady said.

"How long exactly have you had this Detective position? I mean, how long have you been a detective?" Alex asked sarcastically.

Grinning himself, O'Grady said, "Okay, I'll play your game Mr. Rodgers. I've been a detective for about fifteen years."

"And in those fifteen years, how many cases have you solved?"

"Where are you going with this Mr. Rodgers?"

"You see Detective; it's really not my game we're playing here. It's yours. You want to play question and answer with me, so I'm just playing *your* game."

"Look, all I'm doing is asking questions that are puzzling me; you know – ruling out all possibilities. That's all." O'Grady said.

"Well, that makes two of us. I'll tell you what... you answer these last few questions and I'll answer any remaining questions you have."

"I guess; I've solved all but two."

"Okay, final question; in your fifteen years of experience, have you ever run across a case where the boyfriend of a victim didn't have his fingerprints anywhere in the house?" Alex finished sarcastically.

"I see your point Mr. Rodgers, but some of those prints are pretty fresh and in the roommate's room."

"Detective; what kind of idiot do you take me for? I spent four years in the Army, during which, I served as a weapons expert. I also spent two of those years in college studying forensic science. Now, I don't know everything there is to know about forensic science. But I know enough to know that there is no way of telling by your so-called *fresh* prints that I was in that house earlier that morning or five days ago.

"I happen to know that a single fingerprint can survive in one spot for months if it is never disturbed. But it's highly unlikely that one would never be disturbed. But if there were say two, three, five, ten, or twenty people through there, touching anywhere in the vicinity of the area in which you found any one of my prints, then a different print would be left on top of the one of mine that you found. All of which will seemingly be fresh." Alex said, explaining in great detail.

"So please Detective, before you sit me down and ask me stupid questions; you might want to make sure you know the right questions to ask and whom you're asking them to. Another thing Detective, if I was the one that killed those men, you really think I would leave a single print in that house tying it back to me? And as you just said; my fingerprints are all over that house. C'mon Detective... think!" Alex said, getting up from his chair prepared to leave when O'Grady placed his hand against Alex's chest telling him to sit back down.

"You know Detective; I know a few things about the law as I've told you before. Your office or not, unless I'm under arrest, if you don't remove your hand, I am well within my rights to remove it for you and charge you with assault." Alex said sternly as he stared into the eyes of O'Grady.

"You know Mr. Rodgers; something tells me you know more than what you're letting on." O'Grady said as he withdrew his hand quickly.

"Well, you better get a hold of those voices of yours and ask them what it is because I haven't the foggiest clue what the hell you're talking about. If I were you, I'd ask the girls what they know and let us leave. The longer I stay here, the more pissed off I'm becoming. And legally, my friend, I'm not the guy you want to piss off; I'll have your badge so fast; you won't know what hit you." Alex said matter-of-factly as he opened the door, stopping just before he exited the office.

"A piece of advice Detective, the next time you question me or anyone else outside of an interrogation room, I would suggest that you have a witness with you; just to cover your ass." Alex said with a wink.

"Is that a threat, Mr. Rodgers?"

"After everything I've said so far, you're asking if *that* little piece of free advice is a threat... you know, Detective, if you weren't so pathetic or if I were in a better mood, I'd laugh right in your face." Alex stated as he slammed the office door on his way out.

Minutes later, O'Grady opened the door asking Alan Perkins to escort Stephanie into his office and to attend the meeting.

* * *

Ten minutes later, Stephanie came out of the office and Alan went into the next office and escorted Bridget inside shutting the door behind them.

Walking over to where Alex stood by the stairs, Stephanie nestled next to him as he put his arm around her. Within seconds, she was in tears.

"What's wrong, sweetheart?" He asked, stroking her hair.

"I just want to put all of this behind me. O'Grady said they were part of some local gang."

"Did he ask any questions about me?"

"Yeah, he asked if you were there earlier in the day at anytime, then how frequently you visit, what you did for a living, and if I knew whether or not you had ever been in the military." Stephanie said.

"Anything else?"

"He also asked how long we've been together, if you've ever been to college. It's weird, but I think he suspects you." Stephanie finished.

"Did Alan say anything?"

"Yeah, he started to ask the detective why he was asking all these questions about you but O'Grady just blew him off by holding his hand up."

"That's it!" Alex said, pulling his arm back. "Wait here, Bridget will be out in a minute and when I get finished with O'Grady, we'll be leaving."

"Did you know Alex during his tour of service?" Alex heard the detective ask just as he barged into the room.

"Don't answer another question, Bridget." Alex said, opening the door. "Go out and wait with Steph. I want to have a word with the good detective here."

"Mr. Rodgers! What do you think you're doing? You need to leave before I have you arrested." O'Grady said as Bridget got up and left the room.

"Miss Somers, you need to sit back down. I'm not finished."

"The hell you're not!" Alex said. "And what exactly would be the grounds having me arrested Detective? Go ahead Bridget." Alex said.

"How about tampering with an investigation?"

"That might work if I was made known that I was a suspect in this case. And since I haven't, the questions that you're asking these girls about me aren't relevant." Alex said.

Facing Alan, Alex said, "Alan; I want you to witness this."

"Alright Mr. Rodgers, I'll play along. What do you want?" O'Grady asked, sitting back down at his desk.

"I warned you Detective. If you suspect me of something, I suggest you charge me with it right now. Otherwise, I *will* charge you with slander, defamation of character, as well as harassment to not only myself but to those ladies out there. I understand you have a job to do, but unless I'm your *only* suspect, which I know from our conversation at the hospital last night, I'm not; I suggest very strongly that you back the hell off!"

"As you said Mr. Rodgers, I have a job to do and I'm going to do it whether you like the way I do it or not."

"Do you have any evidence showing any possibility of my involvement in the murder of those three individuals?"

"No, not yet, but I will. And when I do; it'll be my pleasure to put you behind bars for the rest of your life." O'Grady said fiercely.

"Well, don't hold your breath. You better come up with some hard evidence to back you or I *will* charge you with those charges and I promise you Detective, they will stick." Alex said, walking out of the office, slamming the door behind him once again.

* * *

"How the hell does he know so much about the law?" O'Grady asked Alan who was sitting rather quietly in one of the chairs by his desk. He had a smug look on his face as if he knew all of what had just happened was going to happen.

"Well, ya see Detective, Alex also took criminal justice and a little law when he was in college. He had a kind of variety of interests inspired mainly by his brother's death. All he really needs to be a certified paralegal is another two years or so." Alan stated.

"He's hiding something and I'm going to find out what it is." O'Grady said.

"Do you want a free piece of advice sir?"

"Everyone's full of advice today. Sure, go ahead."

"If you're going to pursue this, which I recommend that you don't, but if you are, I wouldn't take what Alex says lightly. He doesn't lie, and everything he said that he would do or could do, he *will* do if he's provoked. If you are going to go after him, you better do it by the book. One sway from it and he'll nail you in court. He does know his shit." Alan said as he got up and made his way to the door.

"You act as if he's God all mighty." O'Grady said.

"No, not God per say, do you remember when I told you about Alex's brother?"

"Yes."

"Well, when he was seventeen, Alex had gathered enough evidence on those two dirty cops that let his brother's killer go free that he contacted Internal Affairs with the information. That information not only led to those cops losing their badges but also their freedom. They were each given twenty years for aiding the escape of a murderer and tampering with evidence to try and clear him of the crime. One was killed three days after he hit the yard. The other, well, let's just say that he's making many of the prisoner's stay in prison more bearable." Alan explained.

"So, what are you trying to tell me?"

"I'm trying to tell you that Alex doesn't play games. He means what he says, and he says what he means."

CHAPTER 8

At the insistence of the Chief of Police, the Kansas City Police Department rushed their crime scene team in order to get the bodies of Tulsa's own beloved homicide detectives' home and ready for their funeral.

The funeral was held the morning following Samantha's arrival home and although she didn't feel much like attending a funeral so soon, she was actually happy to get it over and done with.

Each detective received a twenty-one-gun salute for their service. Samantha placed carnations on each coffin and a single white rose across the chest of her long-time friend, partner, and father-figure Dan Riley before it was lowered into the ground.

She had beaten herself up the entire day for not getting to them faster, for not at least warning Dan when she saw the creep come in. The events played over and over in her mind but the more she fretted about it the worse she felt.

As each casket was lowered into the ground, she stayed her salute as if she were a marine soldier waiting for the president himself to tell her to lower it. She had cried all through the night except for the couple of hours that she had been able to sleep. During those hours, the same nightmare plagued her dreams.

After the funeral, she went to the station to fill out her leave papers and to inform Captain Ford of her decision on taking his advice. She told him of the phone call she had received the night before and that she actually might be able to be reunited with her brother sooner than she thought possible.

He was excited for her and wished her well. He, of course, told her that although, he wanted her to still speak with the police psychiatrist, he understood and told her to take as long as she needed and to be rest assured that her job would be waiting for her when she came home.

From the station, she went back to her apartment and gathered a suitcase full of clothes and made sure to pack her gun in the suitcase as well. She knew what Dan would say if he were here, "Kid, you don't need to take your gun with you on vacation."

She chuckled a little under her breath as she thought about that and the response that she would've given, "I take my gun everywhere." It was a running joke that they had shared for years. She carried regardless of where she was or where she was going. Her gun made her feel safe.

At eleven o'clock, Samantha arrived at the airport and approached the ticket counter. "Excuse me; I believe I have a ticket waiting for me. My name is Samantha Elliot." She said to the ticket clerk.

The woman typed on her keyboard and then looked at Samantha. "There seems to be a password protection on this Miss Elliot. Do you happen to know the password?"

"Brunswick."

"Thank you, Miss Elliot, here's your ticket. Will you be checking any luggage?"

"Yes," Samantha replied, putting her suitcase on the lower counter in front of her. "I'm a detective with the Tulsa PD, so I have an unloaded weapon in the bag."

"Okay, may I see your identification for security purposes?"

Samantha pulled a small wallet that bore her Detective badge on the front and showed it to the woman and then flipped it open to reveal her police identification card. "Thank you, Detective Elliot. Are there any other weapons that need to be checked?"

"No, that's the only one. The clips for my gun are in my carry on."

"Okay, I'll place a security sticker on these two bags as well as your carry on which will allow our security guards to know that you're a law enforcement officer and carrying a weapon in your luggage."

"Thank you." Samantha said.

The attendant placed the security stickers and tags on all three of the bags and loaded the suitcases on a conveyer belt to be loaded onto the belly of the plane. "Going to Maine, are you? Summer's definitely the time to go. I hear it's beautiful up there this time of year." The attendant said as she turned back around.

"It is; I'm originally from there; just heading up there for a little reunion." Samantha said.

"That's nice, enjoy your flight."

Finding the terminal rather easily, she looked up at the clock and found that she still had twenty minutes to spare. Going inside of a diner, she ordered a tuna sandwich and a water to drink. As she sat down to eat her sandwich, she saw a man step through the door of the diner. He looked identical to the man from the bar that had taken the life of her friends and whom she had shot dead just less than thirty-two hours ago.

She watched as he approached the counter and placed his right hand in his coat just as the stranger at the bar had done. Samantha's heart jumped in her throat at the sight of this déjàvú but she was determined to find out if the butterflies swarming around in her stomach were indeed a cause for alarm or if paranoia had finally set in.

Slowly getting up from the table, she stepped behind the man wearing the long trench coat. When he spoke, she felt as if she was going to have a heart attack. He sounded exactly like the man that had just recently become a bad memory. As the stranger turned around, Samantha's breath caught in her throat.

She stood staring into those cold dead eyes and watched his lips as they mouthed the words that would haunt her for the rest of her life. But it wasn't just the words; it was the voice. It was Dan's voice not that psycho's that killed him. "Going home Samantha?"

* * *

Samantha snapped her head up from her table with sweat dripping from her face. A server stood over her with her hand lying on Samantha's shoulder, "Are you alright ma'am?"

"What? Who? Where am I?"

"You're at the Air Depot Diner ma'am. Are you alright?"

"I'm fine. I must've dozed off." She said as she looked down at her watch and found that fifteen minutes had elapsed since she walked inside the diner.

Finished with her meal and ready to get going, she left the small diner and walked into one of the many memorabilia stores that were lined all through the airport. Deciding that she needed something to read in order to take her mind off of things, she picked a book written by her favorite author. Some of his stories were a little far-fetched but some actually caught her attention and made her think to herself, "This could actually happen."

This particular novel was one of his most famous 'Good versus Evil' books and was even made into a movie for television in the mid to late Nineties.

Paying six dollars and some change for the novel, she went back to the terminal just in time to hear the counter person call for the First-Class passengers to begin boarding. Getting in line, she handed her ticket to the woman so she could check it.

"You're in First Class section 1 seat A." The woman said.

"Thank you." Samantha said as she boarded the plane and sat in her seat waiting for the rest of the passengers to be seated.

"Would you like something to drink?" A flight attendant asked as she made her rounds.

"No, I'm fine. Thank you." Samantha answered, looking around her section of the plane and taking note of how much nicer it was than Coach.

She wondered how her grandfather had become so wealthy; to afford first class transportation from Oklahoma to Maine. To hire a law firm equipped enough to cut through all the red tape and find her brother. To pass down money as well as property to grandchildren he barely knew. With no strings attached or bills left to pay; it was almost too good to be true.

She sat and pondered for a while and then decided to read her book. Opening the novel, she noticed something out of the corner of her eye. Something that sent cold chills down her spine instantly. A large man sat across the aisle from her and was looking directly at her.

Turning her head to get a better look, the man vanished. Maybe he was never there. Quickly searching the section once more to see if he had moved somewhere else, she found nothing. She was alone in the section.

Deciding that she was just imagining things, she turned her attention back to her novel and began reading. Suddenly, she spotted him again sitting in the very same seat across from her. Quickly turning her head to look at him, he disappeared just as quickly as he had appeared.

"Alright, that's enough of this shit." She said as she got up from her seat.

They had been in the air nearly ten minutes and there were already a lot of people moving about the plane doing various things. Judging by the size of the man she thought she had seen twice; he surely couldn't move all that fast.

She went through every aisle from First Class to Coach, checked what lavatories she could, and even the galley where the flight attendants got all their goodies. Still nothing that even remotely resembled this particular man.

Deciding finally that stress was working overtime on her; she went back to her seat to sit down. When she opened the curtain to return to First Class, however, she noticed a man's arm resting soundly on the armrest of her seat.

Quickening her pace, Samantha rounded the seats and came face to face with the man sitting in her seat. He looked up into her eyes and said, "Watch your back Kid."

P
ulling into his driveway, only thirty minutes after leaving the police station, Alex put the car in PARK and turned to face both girls. "What are we going to do Alex?" Stephanie asked.

Upon leaving the station house, he explained to them what he had discussed with O'Grady in his office when he was questioned and then later when he barged in on Bridget's 'question and answer' session.

"We don't need to do anything." Alex explained.

Stephanie was concerned that they would eventually arrest him for the murder of the men that had attacked them and he knew it.

"Look… O'Grady has absolutely nothing to go on. I was very careful when I was in there and was careful to get rid of the evidence when I left you two on the porch before coming back to the house." Alex continued.

"O'Grady might come up with something eventually, but right now, he has nothing in order to hold me on. By the time he can put anything together to come after me, we'll be long gone." He finished.

"I don't want to be on the run with no where to go." Stephanie said.

"Don't worry, I've got a plan. I'm going to call this Clayton Green, my grandfather's attorney, back and see whether or not I can get any extra money for expenses for the trip up. If I can, we'll head out today." Alex said.

Opening the door, he allowed both of the girls to go in ahead of him. Stephanie kept a few clothes on hand at his place whenever she felt like spending the night or even some weekends with him. They had chosen to wait until they had some more money saved up before getting married so they kept their living arrangements the way they were until then.

Stephanie and Bridget hurried to the back bedroom to get some clothes packed for the trip at hand. Alex asked her to pack a bag for him as well while he made the phone call.

Dialing the number that Clayton Green had given him the night before, Alex waited anxiously but patiently for someone to come on the line. As he waited, he heard something on the front porch. As he started for the door, someone knocked on the door.

With the phone still at his ear listening to the ringing tone that it gave off, Alex opened the door. But when he did, there was no one outside. He pushed the OFF switch on the phone, ending the call that had yet to be answered and stepped out onto the porch to take a look at who could have paid him a visit.

On the porch, just outside the door, lay an envelope with his name written on it. Picking it up to examine it further, he noticed that there was no other writing on the front. No postmark was attached to the envelope either which told him that it was not delivered by a local mail carrier. Whoever had delivered it might actually still be around.

Putting the envelope in his back pocket while still carrying the phone in his left hand, Alex stepped off of the porch and began looking around the yard for anyone who might be lying in wait for him to go back inside so they could leave just as mysteriously as they arrived. Unfortunately, he could find no one or any signs that someone was even there other than he and the girls still inside.

Looking down at the dirt driveway, he couldn't see any other tire marks in the dirt other than the ones he normally made coming in and out. The tracks were all the same.

Pulling the envelope out of his back pocket, stepping back inside the house, Alex stared down at his own name printed neatly in pen on the front of the envelope and wondered what could be inside. In his gut, he had an unnerving feeling that almost brought nausea with it. A cold chill began to run down his back and he shivered and twitched at the feeling.

Finally, turning the envelope over, he opened it and found a note inside tucked into the band of a bundle of hundred-dollar bills. Two simple words struck emotions in Alex's heart that he never thought would: *Love Grandpa.*

Wanting to drop the envelope to the floor out of fear, he held onto it instead out of curiosity and bewilderment. This baffled him more than anything else in his entire life. "How did this get here? Who brought it?"

Undoing the band on the money, he fanned the bills out in order to look at them. He then went to the coffee table sitting in front of the couch and laid the money out on the table in order to count it. When he was finished counting, he had a total of two thousand dollars all in one-hundred-dollar bills.

"How the hell? Where in the world? No, no, I don't even want to know. Thank you, Grandpa. You saved me a phone call." Alex said aloud as he restacked the money and returned it to the envelope

"Who are you talkin' to?" Stephanie said, coming out of the bedroom pulling on a flannel shirt to go with the blue jeans she was already wearing.

"Myself. You won't believe what just happened," he said.

Bridget came out of the room just as he reached the part in his story about the money in the envelope. "Well, let's get going before that idiot detective *does* put two and two together." Bridget said.

"She's right; I don't feel right sticking around here Alex. Detective O'Grady has it in for you, and sooner or later he'll find something to hold you on." Stephanie agreed.

"Well, is there anything that you need before we leave? Another set of clothes or something?" He asked.

"We got everything we need all packed and ready to go." Stephanie said.

* * *

The airport was packed full of people when they arrived in the front lobby. They brought only one suitcase and one carry-on bag so they knew it wouldn't take them too long to get through the lines.

Finding a line with only a few people in it, Alex hurriedly got in and waited his turn at the counter. He had told Stephanie and Bridget to wait on the other side of the metal detectors while he got the tickets so when he joined them, they could go straight to the terminal.

When it was his turn at the counter he said, "Hello."

The ticket counter clerk looked up from her screen and said, "Can I help you?"

"Yes, I have a couple of tickets waiting for me. The name's Rodgers."

Typing his last name into the computer she said, "Alex?"

"Yes ma'am."

"It says here that there is a password identification hold on the tickets. Would you happen to have the password?"

"Brunswick."

"Very good," she said, typing the password into the computer. "It says here that there are two additional tickets being held."

"Two? There should only be one."

Looking down at the screen again, she typed a little more on the keyboard and then looked back at him. "The password was entered earlier this morning at the Tulsa International Airport but only one ticket was taken. If you don't want the other one…"

"No… no, I'll take it." He said, interrupting her.

"Very good; is there any luggage you would like to check in at this time?"

"Just this suitcase and I have one carry-on." He said, pushing the suitcase into the small alcove beside the counter used for loading the luggage belt that would be placed on the plane by airport personnel.

"Are there any breakable items in the suitcase? Any weapons of any kind?"

"No, just clothes."

"The carry-on?"

"Nope, the same."

"Very good," she said, putting a tag on the suitcase indicating his name and destination.

After tagging his luggage and giving him a carry-on tag, she handed him the tickets explaining where they were located and that one of the flight attendants would assist them in seating once they boarded the plane.

Looking down at the tickets, he saw that they were in First Class and he nearly fell over when he saw it. "Are you okay Mr. Rodgers?"

"Yes, just surprised is all."

"Your plane will begin boarding in about six minutes. You will have one layover in Nashville and will change planes there. If you look, you'll see that there is a different color ticket behind each of the ones coming out of here. They will tell you which terminal to head to and the flight number you'll be boarding once you arrive in Nashville." The woman explained.

"Thank you." Alex said, taking the tickets in hand and heading for the metal detectors.

* * *

They boarded the plane at one o'clock and took their seats in First Class. "You know, I thought there would be more to the first-class section than just comfortable seats," Bridget said, "It is nice though."

"I think it's more for the quietness and relaxation than for the nicer accommodations." Alex said.

"More like the first ones to die in a plane crash." Stephanie said shakily.

"Not a good thing to say when you're already on the plane Steph." Bridget said sarcastically.

"Sorry," Stephanie said as the plane began taxiing down the runway getting ready for take off.

Stephanie gripped Alex's hand as they entered the sky. "I really hate flying."

"Nah… I couldn't tell." Alex said as he tried to get circulation back into his hand once the plane leveled off and her grip loosened. "Try to get some sleep sweetheart." Alex said, motioning for a flight attendant. "Could you bring us a couple of pillows and a blanket please?"

"Sure, I'll be right back." The flight attendant said.

A couple of minutes later, she returned, and as she leaned across Alex to place the pillow behind Stephanie's head, he could clearly read her nametag that was attached to her shirt. He found through his education in college that using a person's name as recognition, you tend to get a lot better results than by shouting out, "Hey you!"

"Vanessa, would you mind bringing a pillow and blanket for the young lady sitting behind me as well?" Alex asked, as she stood straight again.

"No problem, sir." Vanessa said, smiling and then left once again.

"Flirt," Stephanie said.

"I am not. I was simply being courteous." Alex rebutted as Stephanie gave a smirk to say, "Yeah right."

Minutes later, Vanessa returned with another pillow and blanket for Bridget. After assisting her with them, she returned to face Alex. "Anything else for you today sir?"

"No, thank you." Alex said as Vanessa took her post again behind the wall where the galley was kept outside the cockpit door.

"You better stop flirting." Stephanie said with a sterner voice.

"I said I'm not flirting honey. I'm just being courteous."

"Whatever!" She said as she lay back and closed her eyes. Within minutes, she was fast asleep.

* * *

At two o'clock the plane landed in Nashville for its thirty-minute layover. They were the first to exit the plane because of their first-class seating and made their way to the gate in which their next flight would be taking off from. The plane had already landed and was in the process of unloading passengers when they arrived.

"I have to go to the bathroom really quick." Stephanie said when they walked past the restrooms.

"Me too," Bridget said, following Stephanie to the restroom.

"Okay," Alex said, "I'll find out when they're going to be loading passengers again."

While he waited for them, he went to the check-in counter beside the terminal doors to find out how long it would be before they started loading the plane again. "In about twenty minutes, sir."

Alex passed her his ticket and she corrected herself, "Oh, you're in First Class… if you give everyone getting off the plane a few minutes, you can board anytime you like."

"Thank you." Alex said, turning and taking a seat as he awaited Stephanie and Bridget to reappear from the restrooms so they could all board together.

Only half a minute passed when he realized that he better use the restroom himself before getting in the air or he'd have to use the closets on the plane the airline called lavatories. Going into the men's room, he relieved himself, washed his hands, and returned to his seat just in time to see Stephanie and Bridget emerge from the lady's room.

Escorting them to the seat in which he had just left, he waited for them to seat themselves and sat between them. "How soon till we can board?" Bridget asked.

"A few more minutes… the attendant asked if we'd give them a few minutes to make sure everyone that is getting off the plane gets off," he said.

Samantha's plane landed in Nashville's airport a little before two o'clock. She was so shaken by the split-second manifestation of her recently deceased partner and best friend, Dan Riley; it was all she could do to get out of her seat to use the facilities the airport provided. The closets they called restrooms the airline provided on their planes had barely enough room to stretch her arms without hitting the walls.

As she stepped off the plane, she noticed the restrooms across the hall from the gate. If no one had been in her way, she would have sprinted there, yet unfortunately, luck would not be on her side. People were everywhere.

Inside the swirling entrance to the restroom, she managed to miss running into two women coming out as she was going in. They both wore no makeup and looked like the devil himself had come up from Hell and slapped them around just for kicks.

One of the women was petite; maybe a hundred and four pounds, with dark brown hair and brown eyes. She had a fair complexion, except for a swollen jaw and dark bruises against her cheeks. Her friend was in similar shape but with not as many bruises; she had dirty blonde hair and a lighter complexion and only a split lip where she looked like she'd been punched.

Her instincts as a police detective wanted to stop and ask them what had happened. But another part of her told her that she was on a different mission and should leave it alone. She let them pass.

When her business was done and her hands were washed; she exited the restroom only to find the same two women sitting outside the restroom at the very gate to her plane. Sitting between them was a man who looked to be in his early to mid twenties. He was wearing blue jeans, a red and black checkered flannel shirt, and a brown leather bomber jacket.

They were talking quietly among themselves when she walked by them and she strained to hear their conversation to please her curiosity. There was something else about the guy; she couldn't quite put her finger on it but he looked very familiar. She glanced back at him several times as she went inside the tunnel of the loading bridge leading to the plane's door, but still couldn't place where she knew him from.

* * *

On the plane, trying desperately to relax, Samantha felt uneasy. She kept thinking about the man sitting with those two women. She was certain that she'd never met him but was certain that she knew him.

Minutes passed and the plane started to be boarded by passengers. The first to enter the plane were none other than the two women she had passed going into the restroom and the man that had been sitting between them. They took a seat in the First-Class section with her. The man and the dirty blonde sat across from her and the brunette ended up sitting right beside her. Samantha was sitting in the aisle seat, so the brunette had to climb over to get to the window seat.

A few minutes later, more people began boarding, rushing past them into Coach. Once everyone was seated, the flight attendant came over the intercom and began her normal routine pre-flight speech. Samantha, however, kept glancing over at the guy sitting across the aisle with the dirty blonde.

She tried not to stare because she didn't want the woman sitting with him or the woman sitting beside her to get suspicious and get the wrong idea. She had thought several times just to come out and ask the guy his name, hoping that it would jog her memory so she could place him, but then thought better of it. She didn't know how she would be able to make it sound like a casual conversation starter and not an interrogation.

Choosing to finally look away from the guy, determined to listen to the pre-flight instructions instead, she stared at the flight attendant giving the speech and thought to herself how monotonous it would be to have that job.

From the seat behind her she heard a voice say, "Oh come on Kid. This would be the perfect job for you."

Sitting frozen in her seat, knowing that her eyes must be as big around as silver dollars, she forced herself to turn to look at the man behind that voice. When she turned in her seat, he found herself looking into the face of a man that looked identical to Dan Riley. It had to be a different man. Dan Riley was dead and buried. It had to be a doppelganger.

"What did you say?" She whispered to the man seated behind her. The man leaned forward in his seat and peered directly into Samantha's eyes.

"You heard me Kid. You're not imagining things, I *am* here. Somebody's gotta have your back."

* * *

"Are you okay, ma'am?" The flight attendant asked after completing her demonstration.

Turning to face the flight attendant once more, she said, "Is there anyone sitting behind me?"

"No ma'am. Are you okay?"

"I don't know. I may just be tired. Could you bring me a pillow and a blanket?" She said, hoping that no one else saw that she was talking to thin air just a moment before.

"Sure, I'll be right back."

"Quit fighting Kid. You'll be happy later that I'm here." The voice said this time sitting beside her in the very seat that the brunette had just occupied.

Samantha tried to ignore the voice as she anxiously awaited the flight attendant's return. Looking over to the seat across from her, she saw the sitting with the blonde woman staring at her.

The look on his face was pale, as if he'd seen a ghost, and he started to say something to her but stopped short when the flight attendant arrived with her blanket and pillow.

Taking the objects from her; she looked away from the guy sitting across from her with a smile and reluctantly faced the direction where the voice had come from the second time. Miraculously, the brunette was seated there once again. Samantha closed her eyes, put the pillow behind her head and nestled against it, and pulled the blanket over her shoulders, tucking her chin beneath the blanket and quickly fell asleep.

* * *

Blood... There was blood everywhere. Blood ran down the stairwell forming a small puddle at the bottom of the stairs. At the top of the stairwell lay a body of a woman; a woman covered in blood. Thunder echoed outside and lightning flashed through the windows illuminating briefly the dark upstairs hallway, revealing the shadows of death. Glowing eyes in the darkness, like that of a cat about to pounce upon its prey, frightened her because she knew that they belonged to a far more sinister predator.

She woke from her nightmare with a jolt and struck out with her fist, just as a hand snatched her wrist before contact with anything or anyone could be made. She opened her eyes to see the mystery man she had been trying to recognize, standing over her and holding her wrist in one hand while shaking her other arm with his other, trying to bring her around.

The girl who had been sitting beside her had changed seats to where she was now sitting behind the dirty blonde. How she had managed that without waking her, she had no idea.

"Are you okay?" He asked with general concern.

"Yeah; just a nightmare. I'm fine now."

"I'd say you were having a nightmare. You were flailing around here like something was attacking you. You have nightmares like this often?"

"Only when I sleep," she said, trying to laugh off the incident. "Sorry if I disturbed you."

"No problem… I uhhh… saw you looking my direction earlier, but my girlfriend thought you were looking at her. She said she saw you coming into the restroom back at the airport as she and her friend were going out. She said you kinda freaked them out when you stared at them. I told them they were just being paranoid."

"I'm sorry. I *was* actually looking at you."

"Me? Why?"

"I was trying to place where I'd seen you before. Or at the very least, try to think if I knew someone that looked like you. I do that often when something begins to bug me. Sometimes if I look at whatever it is puzzling me long enough, it'll pop in my head. But for some reason, I'm drawing a blank on you. I just can't place where I've seen you before. But I *am* sorry if it bothered you."

"No bother. What were you dreaming about?" The man replied, sitting back down in his seat across from her.

"A house," Samantha said.

"A house…? All that thrashing about over a house?" The man said jokingly, yet with a baffled look on his face.

"Not just any house. I've never been there before, that I know of, but I can describe it to a tee. I believe someone was killed in that house. I saw blood everywhere in my dream."

"I'm sure it was just a run-of-the-mill nightmare. You're reading too much into it."

"I'd normally agree with that assumption except for one thing… this isn't the first time I've had this dream." Samantha argued. "But I'm okay, thanks for waking me. Again, I'm sorry if I bothered you Mister… uhhh…"

"Rodgers… Alex Rodgers."

The shocked look on the woman's face seated across from him when he mentioned his name startled even him. Alex had woken her from what apparently was a nightmare because of the way she was thrashing about in her seat and nearly hitting Bridget in the face. Bridget had carefully climbed over the woman and quickly moved to the seat directly behind Stephanie that was empty.

When the woman explained that she was having a nightmare and elaborated a little on the context of that nightmare, it seemed that – to him – she had been living it literally and was suffering from a repressed memory rather than a dream.

"Are you going to be okay?" He asked again with true concern for the woman.

Instead of answering his question she said, "Let me ask you something; if you have a minute."

"Sure."

"Are you from Georgia?"

"Well, you can pretty much tell that by my accent. What are you really trying to ask me?"

"Okay… How about this one? Are you flying to Maine to see a man named Clayton Green?"

"Okay, now you're startin' to scare me. Who are you, some kind of psychic? The only people that know where I'm going are my girlfriend, her friend, Clayton Green, and my…" Alex answered with a surprised look on his face as he realized who this woman must be; "sister… Samantha?"

"Oh my God!" The woman shouted as she released her seatbelt and thrust her arms around him with tears rolling down her face.

The flight attendant that had given the woman a pillow and blanket earlier approached asking if everything was alright.

"Everything's fine." She said finally releasing Alex from her embrace.

Stephanie stared at the woman, astonished at the suddenness of her embrace of her boyfriend. She quickly realized, though, of who she must be, when Alex said her name.

"I knew I'd seen you before, but I never would have imagined after all this time I would be seeing my baby brother again." Samantha said.

* * *

The hours passed by so quickly that Samantha hadn't realized she and her brother had managed to talk through the entire remaining time of the trip. When the Captain came over the intercom system for them to return to their seats and fasten their seatbelts, she realized what they needed to do next once they landed.

In the short amount of time they had talked, she had found out a lot about her brother and his life. He had explained who the women with him were, but it seemed that he was holding something back. She had told him of Dan and her relationship with him. She told how she had lost him to a maniac with a gun and how she had taken out that same maniac in order to save her own life. She refrained, however, from informing Alex about the hallucinations of Dan, she had been having since she stepped foot on the plane.

"Do you know where you're staying tonight?" Alex said.

"I'm staying at the Holiday Inn just as soon as I can get a rental car... you?"

"Actually, I don't know. I haven't made any accommodations anywhere yet."

"You better hope they're not all booked up." She said quickly.

"Well, I guess I could call up where you're staying and see if they have anything left."

"That would be a smart thing to do," she said.

"Look at you, not my big sister again but five minutes and already lecturing me." Alex joked.

"Not yet, I haven't. You just wait, I get worse." Samantha joked as the plane taxied to the gate where they would depart.

"Are you sure you're my sister?" Alex joked in return.

* * *

When they were inside the terminal and getting their bags from the conveyer belt, Alex told Stephanie that he was going to see if he could get them a room where Samantha was staying. She stayed behind waiting for their suitcase with Bridget and he quickly went on his way.

With the suitcase in hand, Stephanie and Bridget walked over to a diner to wait for Alex. Samantha joined them once she picked up her suitcase and procured a rental car for the trip the following morning. She had decided that they take just one vehicle and insisted that she pay the cost of the rental. Alex had argued of course, mainly because he had that extra cash that had mysteriously arrived on his front porch earlier that same day, but Samantha wouldn't listen.

When she arrived in the diner, she saw both women sitting at a table in front of the window where Stephanie could see Alex. They were just to the right of the entrance and she stepped over to the table.

"Mind if I sit down?" She asked.

"Sure. So; you're a boy in blue; well girl in blue I should say. Huh?" Stephanie said as Samantha took a seat across the table.

"Yeah, I'm a detective actually with the Tulsa Police Department." Samantha said.

"Do you like it? Being a detective, I mean." Bridget asked.

"It has its ups and downs. You heard what happened to my partner…"

"Yeah, I'm so sorry." Stephanie said. "So… this news about your grandfather couldn't have come at a worse time, huh?"

"Actually, it couldn't have come at a better time. If things hadn't gone down the way they did or had gone another way, I wouldn't be here right now. I try to look on the bright side of things; I've learned to do that over the years."

"Why? What happened to make you start doing that?" Bridget asked.

"Well, after my parents died and my brother was taken from me, I felt I had nothing else to live for. When I was finally adopted, my adoptive parents, Matthew and Laura Ellis, loved me from the start and tried to show me that life was worth living. They had such an upbeat on life that it kind of took hold on me after a while and I took to the same idea.

"It took me about two or three years to get over my parents' death and the loss of my brother, but my new parents stuck with me and helped me through it. From that point on, I've tried to look on the brighter side of things."

"That's deep." Bridget said.

"So, tell us about your partner. How did you come to meet him; to know him?"

"Dan was a great guy. He was the first one to befriend me when I arrived at the department. I was still pretty young and had made detective faster than ninety percent of the men there."

"That's showing them!" Bridget said with excitement.

"Shhh!" Stephanie whispered.

Giggling a little under her breath, she continued, "Anyway, Dan wouldn't let the guys pick on me too much. He had ten years seniority over most of them and a good deal of experience over me. He was very good at his job; solid as a rock. But he cared about *his* people; meaning those of us under him."

"Sounds like a good guy." Stephanie said.

"No, he was a great guy. The night he died, he and some of the guys hog-tied me and dragged me clear to Kansas City, to a bar owned and run by his sister for my birthday."

"You mean; he died on your birthday?" Bridget gasped.

"Yeah; anyway, everything I had that night was on the house, so I was drinking some mixed drinks. Hell, I never even got a buzz. All the guys had beer and were toasted. When I got up to go to the restroom, I saw this guy walk into the bar dressed mainly in all black wearing a black duster or trench coat.

"He looked kinda odd so I asked Dan to get me a drink at the bar while I went to the restroom. I actually wanted to get a better look at this guy and wanted Dan closer to back me up if need be. I really didn't need to pee so while I was in there, I kept the door open a crack. I could hear everything. Dan had to be shit-faced because he didn't pick up on any unusual behavior from this guy.

"I heard the stranger raising his voice; sounding really agitated. I pulled and cradled my sidearm and…"

"You *weren't* on duty. Why'd you have your gun?"

"I'm on duty all the time, twenty-four-seven. Besides, I was supposed to work that day. Anyway, I drew my gun when I heard a *click* sound. I found out later that the sound was from a pump action shotgun and the man had pumped the gun to charge it. Everything went fast from there. When the smoke cleared, I was the only one standing. The stranger had killed everyone in the bar except me and I put one bullet between his eyes."

"So, Dan gave his life for you." Stephanie said.

"No, Dan didn't get a chance to *give* his life for me. The bastard took his life… then I took his."

* * *

Alex booked two rooms at the Holiday Inn, one for he and Stephanie and one for Bridget. They all needed a good night sleep especially after what the girls had already been through and he figured this would be the best place.

He began making his way to the diner when he noticed a man in his mid-twenties dressed in a black trench coat, black jeans, and a black shirt. As he walked into the diner behind the man, Alex remembered what Samantha had told him about the man that had shot and killed her partner. The similarity of her description and the appearance of this man were uncanny. Alex decided to watch this guy carefully as he too entered the diner.

Stephanie, Bridget, and Samantha were sitting at a table just to the right of the door. They were deep in conversation as Alex approached the table.

"This seat taken?" He asked as he took a seat beside Samantha.

"Well, it is now cowboy." Stephanie said with a wink. "We all set up for rooms?"

"Yeah, I got one for us and one for Bridget. When we eat, we'll head on over." Alex said.

"Samantha was just telling us more about herself and what happened to her partner…" Stephanie said eager to hear the rest of the story.

"Well, don't let me interrupt." Alex said, settling into the seat to listen as well.

* * *

As Samantha continued telling her story, Alex scanned the diner looking for the stranger in black he had walked in behind. Keeping in mind that his sister was a cop; he tried to be discreet so she wouldn't pick up on what he was doing and overreact if she saw the guy.

"What's wrong Alex?" Stephanie asked, interrupting the story.

"Nothing; just looking for our waitress. Damn the service is lousy here." Alex replied, keeping his true intention secret for now.

"I believe this is a do-it-yourself place. You gotta go up and order what you want at the register. Then someone will be around to deliver it when it's done." Samantha said.

"Damn… the service is lousier than I thought." Alex said, getting up from the table. "I'm gonna go get something to eat. Any of you want anything?"

"I'm fine…" Bridget said.

"Me too," Stephanie said.

"Yeah, I'm good too." Samantha said, returning to her story.

Alex found the stranger in black standing at the counter. He stepped behind the man and waited in line. He wanted to see what the stranger was going to do. The stranger put his hand inside his coat, looked around the diner, and then faced the kid at the counter. Alex could hear the teenage boy behind the counter ask for the stranger's order but heard nothing from the man in black.

Approaching cautiously behind the man, Alex could hear the kid still asking whether or not he could help him. Still; the stranger said nothing. He just stared at him with a blank stare.

"Sir… sir; you're gonna have to order something. You're holding up my line."

Alex reached his hand out to tap the stranger on the back of the shoulder, but when he went to tap him, only air stood between him and the kid behind the counter.

"Sir… can you hear me?" The boy repeated for the third time and Alex finally realized that the kid was talking to him not the man who he thought was standing in front of him.

"I'm sorry…" Alex said. "I guess I was daydreaming."

Birds... No, not just birds... crows. Crows circled above the huge and eerie house. Clouds that seemed to be growing darker and darker; rolled across the sky building more and more moisture for the time to be right for them to explode and release a downpour.

Darkness had already taken over the day and lightning clashed across the sky to reveal shadows of those crows circling overhead across the ground. Thunder boomed within seconds after the lightning with a loud crackling sound.

The door to the house stood open. Inside, lay clothes scattered along the foyer floor like torn paper. At the foot of the staircase pooled a tiny puddle of blood as it flowed down the stairs like water.

At the top of the stairs lay the body of a woman brutally murdered and stripped of her dignity. Matted bloody hair covered her face, concealing her identity. Then suddenly the hair moved away from her face, revealing a pair of pale blue eyes staring blindly into the darkness. Aside from the blood smeared all over the woman's face and the look of terror painted across it, the face of the woman was a complete mirror image of her own.

Waking and gasping for air, Samantha sat up straight in her bed. The vivid image in her mind scared her even now, though she was awake. She screamed an eardrum-shattering scream that could easily have woken even the dead and within minutes brought pounding to her door.

Getting up from her bed, shaking her head violently to loosen the image from her mind, she approached the door and peered through the peephole. Outside, a man dressed in a pair of sweat pants and t-shirt insistently pounded on her door.

"I'm okay, I'm okay. I just had a nightmare. Thank you for your concern." Samantha said, opening her door.

"Are you sure?" The man asked as a woman came out of the room across the hall, pulling a complimentary robe over her nightgown.

"Yes, I'm sure. Thank you." Samantha said again as she shut her door.

* * *

Crows, Crows flying overhead, circling, and soaring through the sky. The road was long and winding with tall trees all around. Ahead there was something in the road… a deer? No, too large for a deer. A bear? No, too large to be a bear. Coming closer… closer… a moose. A moose stood in the middle of the road.

Rain began to fall just as lightning raced across the sky trying to beat the thunder to its mutual destination. The moose stood still for a couple of seconds with the headlights from the car shining brightly into its eyes. The reflection from the lights gave a look of satanic possession across the face of the huge beast. Finally, the moose finished making its way across the road.

Further down the road, another object appeared in the road; this time much smaller than a moose. The silhouette resembled that of a man. As the shadowy figure came closer into view, it revealed itself to be a man about five-eleven maybe six feet tall and of a thin to medium build; stocky in the chest and shoulders. He was dressed in black from head to toe. He wore a black overcoat and a hat to keep the rain from wetting his clothes.

He too was black with a touch of Native American blood, for he was not of a very dark complexion. His hair was long and was pulled back into what appeared to be several braids known in the African-American community as 'dreadlocks.' He stood very calmly along the side of the road as rain beat down atop his head, waiting for someone to stop and give him a ride.

Coming to a stop beside the dark stranger, Alex rolled down the passenger side window to ask if the stranger needed a ride. But when he peered out into the rain filled day, the only thing standing outside the door was a mailbox fastened atop a tree trunk. Perched atop that mailbox was a single crow, staring back into his eyes. It cawed into the darkness and then flew away into the rainy sky.

With the sound of screams coming from the next room, Alex woke from his disturbing dream and quickly got out of bed. Stephanie was already up and pulling a complimentary robe over her bare body. Alex quickly exited his door and used the extra key card he had for Bridget's door to enter her hotel room.

There he found Bridget lying sprawled across the bed, beside her bed stood a man in his late twenties-early thirties with his shirt completely bloody. His arms and hands were painted in blood. He stood over Bridget but was not touching her. In his hand, he held an eight-inch blade with blood dripping from it.

Wasting no time, Alex ran into the room and leaped across the bed to tackle the blood-soaked stranger. But in his place, he tackled only the nightstand and lamp, knocking them over and bloodying his own lip in the process.

Getting to his feet, Alex quickly scanned the room for his lightning quick opponent but found no one except for Stephanie who was now standing in the doorway and Bridget sitting up in her bed.

* * *

Samantha glanced at the complimentary alarm clock that the hotel provided in most all the rooms and found it to be five thirty in the morning. She knew there was no way she was going to get back to sleep. She decided instead to take a shower and try to clear the images of the nightmare from her mind.

Gathering some clothes, she began making her way into the bathroom when she felt a slight breeze sweep through the room. She shivered. Trying to ignore her own instincts to get the hell out of the room, she turned and went into the bathroom anyway. Turning the water on to allow it to reach the proper temperature, she heard the phone ringing beside the bed. Turning the knob to activate the showerhead, she returned to the bed and picked up the receiver.

"Hello."

"Don't go near the Brunswick House if you know what's good for you." A raspy deep throated voice said on the other end.

* * *

"Are you alright Bridget?" Alex asked when he was sure that they were the only ones in the room.

"Yeah, but maybe I should be asking you that." Bridget said.

"I'm fine. Why were you screaming?"

"I was screaming?"

"Yeah, I'd say you were screaming!" Stephanie said, entering the room. "You scared the shit out of us."

"I'm sorry. If I was screaming; I can't remember."

"Well, you were screaming like someone was attacking you." Alex said, setting the nightstand back where it had been before he pummeled it.

"Maybe I was dreaming about what happened," she said, referring to the ordeal back in Georgia. "I don't know, I truly don't remember."

"It's okay." Stephanie said as she sat on the edge of the bed and wrapped her arms around her friend.

"Um... Alex... Why were you playing Superman just then?" Bridget said, releasing Stephanie from her embrace.

"Oh that... I thought I saw someone in the shadows. You woke me from a really weird dream."

"What was your dream about?" Stephanie asked.

"Well let's go down to breakfast since we're up and I'll tell you all about it."

* * *

Samantha walked into the hotel restaurant located downstairs from her room about five minutes to six and sat down at the nearest table to the door. Within minutes, a waitress came by offering her a cup of coffee.

"Sure... Could I get some creamer and extra sugar please?" She said, accepting the coffee and a menu.

"No problem. I'll be right back." The waitress said, walking away.

She began to look at her menu when she noticed Alex, Stephanie, and Bridget walk into the restaurant. "Mind if we sit down?" Alex asked, taking a seat across from her.

"I guess so." Samantha said allowing, Bridget to sit in the seat beside her by the wall.

"So, what are you doing up so early?" Alex asked.

"Had a nightmare and couldn't get back to sleep." Samantha said.

"Me too; what was yours about?" Alex replied.

"Well, it involved crows."

* * *

Samantha ended her story with the disturbing phone call she had received before taking her shower.

"That is weird." Stephanie said.

Alex in turn told the story of his dream and ended with the events that had taken place in Bridget's room only minutes earlier. He also included the description of the man he had seen standing over Bridget moments before he tackled the nightstand.

"Something really weird is going on." Bridget said after Alex had finished his story.

"You think?" Stephanie said sarcastically.

"You don't have to be a smart ass." Bridget said.

Before Stephanie could reply, Alex spoke up, "C'mon girls, we got enough problems here without you two fighting."

"You're right, I'm sorry." Stephanie said.

"It's alright. I forgive you." Bridget said.

"Well, I don't know about you three but I want to get to the bottom of this. This nightmare has been plaguing my dreams for far too long now. I'm not about to turn tail and run either." Samantha said.

"Well, I agree. I've never run away from anything either and I'm not about to start now." Alex said.

Detective O'Grady had visited the home of Alex Rodgers several times during the course of the past twenty-four hours in order to question him further on his possible involvement in the homicides that had taken place at his girlfriend's home. He had the forensics team separate the fingerprints found in the two rooms via computer technology and was still convinced that he was involved with the unjustified homicides of those three men.

As far as he was concerned, anyone who took the law in their own hands was no better than the criminals that committed the act they were avenging. Alex Rodgers may be one of the good guys but O'Grady was convinced he was lying about being there before the police had arrived.

The prints, however, didn't show how long before or after each was placed before the other. Alex Rodgers had been right about that. But there had to be something else he was missing and needed to speak with Alex one more time.

He was hoping if he kept on him, sooner or later, Alex would slip up and say something that would provide him with the hard evidence O'Grady need to put him away. Unfortunately, Alex Rodgers along with both women had disappeared. The only place he had left to look; he realized should've been his first stop… the airport.

* * *

At nine o'clock Detective O'Grady arrived at the Atlanta International Airport. Pulling his unmarked sedan to the curb for departing passengers, he parked. Just as he was getting out of the cruiser, a baggage attendant started to approach him but he quickly flashed his badge and the guy returned to what he was doing.

Entering the airport's main entrance, he flashed his badge to everyone standing in his way as he approached the ticket counter. He knew showing photographs would be a waste of time. Airline employees usually see millions upon millions of people a day; they would not be able to recognize anyone by a simple picture.

When the ticket counter attendant looked up from her computer screen O'Grady knew just what to say, "Hello… My name's Detective Marshall O'Grady, I'm investigating a case and I need some help."

"What can I help you with Detective?"

"Well, I need to know if a few people have boarded any flights in the past twenty-four to thirty-two hours by any of these names…" O'Grady said, listing off the names of Alex Rodgers and the women that accompanied him.

"Just a moment," The attendant said as she turned to her computer.

"Yes sir, all three boarded a flight yesterday afternoon for Bangor, Maine."

"Bangor, Maine?" O'Grady said. "I wonder what they're doing there."

* * *

Alan Perkins quickly made his way to the airport the moment that he was called by Detective O'Grady. Alan was new to the detective game. Although he was a Sergeant; he lacked the experience that came with detective work. He had earned his stripes due to prior military experience in the field of Law Enforcement combined with his current work on the force.

Detective O'Grady's rank was that of a Lieutenant but he preferred the title of 'Detective' to that of 'Lieutenant' when being addressed and Alan reluctantly obliged. Arriving at the airport at nearly nine forty-five in the morning, O'Grady was standing outside, at his car, waiting for him.

"Sgt. Perkins, you'll never guess where your boy is." O'Grady said as Alan approached him from his own car.

"Well, Detective, considering that we're at the airport; I'd say he's out of state." Alan said sarcastically.

"Funny; try Bangor, Maine. Do you have any idea why he would be going to Maine?"

"Not really; vacation maybe. You never told him that he couldn't leave town."

"Didn't I?"

"No sir, you threatened to nail his ass to the wall once you found the evidence you needed, but you never mentioned that he couldn't go anywhere."

"Well, I meant to – doesn't matter though – you're gonna get your first piece of detective work Sergeant. I want you on the next flight to Bangor."

"I'm not payin' for a ticket to Maine!" Alan exclaimed.

"You don't have to. It's on the department. Just tell the woman at the ticket counter who you are, provide the proper identification, and inform her that you are going to Bangor to escort a prisoner back."

"Is he under arrest?"

"No, dummy… not yet anyway. I need him back here for questioning."

"What about my weapon?"

"I can tell you've never crossed state lines before to chase a suspect. When you show them your badge to get your ticket, let them know that you're an armed police officer and they'll place a note on your ticket and on the affidavit showing that you're armed. I want you to call me when you arrive in Maine." O'Grady said.

"Yes sir."

At twelve o'clock, they arrived at the offices of **CLAYTON AND GREEN AND ASSOCIATES**, located in downtown Augusta. Alex took a breath, let it out in a gasp, and looked over at his sister who had mimicked him. "Let's do this." He said, leading the way to the office doors.

Opening the door, he held it for each of the girls as they went inside; Samantha leading the way. Directly inside the door was a receptionist desk. Sitting behind the desk, was a beautiful brown-haired woman wearing a headset atop her head answering phones.

Stephanie and Bridget took seats provided directly across from the receptionist desk. Alex and Samantha, however, stood silently in front of the woman's desk waiting for her to look up at them. Thirty seconds later, the woman took her headset off, straightened her hair back with one hand, and then looked at them both.

"Hello, can I help you?" The woman said with a smile on her face.

"We're here to see Mr. Clayton Green." Alex said.

"Your names?"

"Alex Rodgers…"

"Samantha Elliot." Samantha said, finishing the introduction.

"One moment, please." The woman said as she pushed a couple of buttons on her phone then looked back at them, "Would you care to have a seat, it might be a minute."

They took the woman's advice and took a seat on either side of Stephanie and Bridget. A couple of seconds later, the receptionist got up from behind her desk and walked to the back of a hallway immediately to her left.

"Apparently, no one's answering." Alex mumbled.

Minutes later she returned and asked them to follow her.

* * *

Inside Clayton Green's office, Alex and Samantha each took a seat in front of a vacant desk. Before their escort left, she told them that Clayton Green would be with them shortly.

Only five minutes had passed when the door opened once again and a tall burly haired man with a thin build stepped into the office. He was wearing a blue suit and a white starched shirt with a dark blue tie neatly centered under his collar. He had a beard that was not too long; barely off the chin. He stood about six-two and had brown hair. His beard, on the other hand, had a reddish tint to it revealing the Irish blood in him.

"I'm Clayton Green." The man said, shaking hands with both of them. "You must be Alex and Samantha."

"Yes." Alex confirmed.

"Can I offer either of you a cup of coffee... soda... water?" Clayton asked before sitting.

"No, I think we're alright." Alex answered.

"Okay then, let's get down to business." Clayton said, pulling a file out of his file cabinet before finally taking a seat behind his big oak desk.

"Well, to make a long story short, your grandfather was extremely wealthy. In the last decade of his life; he had purchased an old house just north of Rockland, between the towns of Rockport and Camden."

"Wait a minute," Samantha interrupted. "I remember a little about my grandfather before we were sent back to Social Services and were adopted. I don't remember him being wealthy."

"You're right; Mr. Stevenson was just a normal run of the mill lobsterman until he became the sole winner of the Maine lottery. He chose to take the cash and invest it. After a few years, his winnings tripled. After a few more years, it grew more."

"That explains it." Alex said, trying to get the lawyer back to the story.

"Anyway… the house is set off in the country, deep into the woods. There is a road that you can take off the main highway to get to it but it turns into a dirt road after a few miles. The house was built by a carpenter by the name of Tom Brunswick… hence the name of the house. He had built the house to live in with his wife, Annie, soon after they had married. It had been nearly completed when a most unfortunate and terrible thing happened…"

Suddenly a buzzer from the phone sounded, startling nearly all of them. Pressing the button he said, "Not now Melissa, I'm in the middle of a meeting."

"I know sir; it won't take but a minute." The woman said. Alex and Samantha looked at one another, wondering silently if that would be the receptionist's name.

"Excuse me for a moment." Clayton Green said, getting up from his desk and stepping back through the door.

"I'm really intrigued by this story." Alex said, looking over at his sister sitting beside him.

"Me too, I wonder what happened?" Samantha said just as Clayton Green appeared through the door once more and took a seat behind his desk once more.

"I'm sorry about that, where was I?"

"An unfortunate thing happened…." Alex reminded him anxious to hear the rest of the story.

"Oh yes, an unfortunate thing happened… A man, who to this day has yet to identified, broke into the house one stormy morning and killed them both. Apparently, Tom Brunswick had managed to fight back a little though. There were several signs of a struggle – rumpled sheets in the master bedroom, blood droplets in the room leading back into the main hall to the head of the stairs, and finally broken pegs along the staircase indicating that someone had fallen down the stairs.

"Tom and his wife were found nearly three days later decomposing in their own home. A paperboy of all people found the bodies and reported them to the police. Tom and his wife had died from being stabbed to death by a knife. In those days, forensics in this state was damn near a rumor in medical science, yet the doctor that investigated the scene *was* very good.

He concluded that the knife wound had eventually ruptured his kidney and Tom had bled to death.

"The report also showed that Annie had been the first victim in this tragedy. She had been savagely torn apart by this monster… blood had been found running down the staircase as if it were water." Clayton Green continued.

"After the mess had finally been cleaned up, none the family of either victim could be found in order to notify and eventually, the city took possession of the house. A young couple purchased it in an auction several months later and completed the house. They eventually heard of the story behind the house, though the realtor was trying desperately to keep that news from them. They felt so sorry for the couple that had died in that house that they decided to name the house after them."

"That was nice of them." Samantha said.

"The couple only lived in the house a few years before they started experiencing strange things."

"What kind of things?" Alex asked.

"They claim that the house was haunted by its former owners; Tom and Annie Brunswick. They sold the house to a man out of Connecticut nearly five years after they abandoned it."

"Did he have any similar experiences?" Samantha asked.

"As a matter of fact, he did. He claims that many times when it rained outside, he could hear someone knocking at the door. But when he went to investigate, there wouldn't be anyone outside. Several times while he would be out in the backyard for one reason or another, he said he saw a man running into the woods holding the side of his neck."

"Anything else?" Alex asked.

"Oh yes… he also claims to hear a man crying at the head of the stairs but when he goes to check it out… there's nothing."

"How long did he stay in the house?" Alex asked again.

"He put up with the strange occurrences for another two years or so before he couldn't take it anymore. At the end, he told the realtor that the spirits in the house were becoming increasingly violent. He left the house in the reality's capable hands and was sold within three years to your grandfather."

"Wow… did he know what he was purchasing?" Samantha asked, beating Alex to the punch.

"Actually, the reality company had had so many problems with the house and getting buyers, they decided to tell him from the beginning what problems the house possessed. No pun intended. Your grandfather literally jumped at it. He paid the price they wanted and even threw in a little extra to close the house quickly."

"When did he do this? I remember when we lived with him, as short a time it was, and I don't remember this house." Samantha said.

"According to your grandfather, he purchased the house nearly two full years after his stroke. He had a carpenter friend of his check out the place after he bought it to see what it would take to bring the house back and he paid it."

"Did he say whether or not, he had any problems in the house?" Alex asked.

"According to him, he didn't have one single problem. He did have similar experiences as the others that had lived there but he said he was not terrified. He enjoyed the drama."

"He must've had some dark sense of humor." Alex said.

"On the contrary… he claimed that the drama kept him going for more than ten years. When he was diagnosed with cancer, he decided to look for a way to keep the house within his family. He knew that you two had been adopted but didn't know where you had been placed. He contracted my office to search for you by any means necessary and paid us well to find you. He made up his will and made sure that in the event of his death that I personally would carry out his final wishes and bring you two together."

"How did you hear of all of these stories?" Samantha asked.

"Well, when your grandfather hired me and told me what he wanted, he made sure to tell me the entire history of the house, as he knew it, so that I could relay it to you when the time came."

"I see. You also said something about an inheritance on top of this house," Samantha said.

"Yes, by all means, here you are." The tall man said, pulling two checks from the manila folder in front of him and handed one to each of them. "You may cash them or whatever you like at the Credit Union where Mr.

Stevenson's account is located. The name of the Credit Union is on the checks."

Alex looked down at his check and was rewarded with a number he never thought would ever exist in his lifetime. Twelve point five million dollars was written on his check. He sat in awe until he looked at his sister sitting beside him and found that her eyes were as big as half dollars as she stared at the number on her check. She didn't blink one time.

"The house belongs to both of you. Once you look at it, you can decide what you want to do with it. Just let me know by the end of the month so I can draw up the paperwork. You will both need to sign your names before anything can be done with it."

"Can you give us directions to the house?" Samantha finally asked as she shook the half dollar eyes away from her face.

"Sure. Let me have my secretary print you out a map from here to Rockland. From there, she'll write the directions down for you to follow so you can reach the house."

* * *

Within ten minutes they were all out of Augusta and were back on the road. With the directions given to them by Melissa, Clayton Green's secretary, they were directed through not one but two rotary roads and onto Highway 9 heading south. At the first set of lights, they came to, they followed the directions and turned left heading east down Highway 17.

The directions told them to follow Highway 17 until they arrived in Rockland where they would then take Route 1 north about 10 more miles where there would be a Convenience store on the left. The road leading to the house was supposed to be between five and ten miles from there.

Alex had explained to Stephanie and Bridget what was said in Clayton Green's office. Their eyes widened at the story of the house but their mouths dropped open at the mention of the amount of money that both he and Samantha had received.

Twenty minutes on the road, listening to the local country music radio station, they became tired of the noise and Alex turned it off. They continued their conversation about the house as Samantha drove. From overhead, clouds began to roll in from the south and west of them.

Soon, the sun became a memory as rain began to plummet against the roof of the car, seeming to grow in size and intensity as each drop fell. Lightning shot steaks across the sky as the wind began to pick up outside the car windows, causing a spooky howling sound to pass through the glass of each window and sending vibrations with them that they could each feel all the way to the marrow.

"What the hell?" Samantha said. "Alex, do you see what I see up ahead?"

"Do I have to see what you're seeing? I was just fine not seeing that crow on that sign up there." Alex replied.

"Good, at least I'm not going crazy." She said as she neared the sign at a faster rate than she would have liked.

Approaching the sign at fifty-five miles an hour, the sign and crow metamorphosed into a man who was standing along the side of the road. He had muscular shoulders and arms but was somewhat hidden beneath a long body length black overcoat. Atop his head, he wore a hat with a brim that surrounded his head.

The man was of a dark complexion, most likely of an African-American and Native American descent and was dressed entirely in black as well. He had shoulder-length hair pulled back and braided into dreadlocks. Simultaneously, Alex and Samantha gasped in surprise. They had both seen this man before.

"Stop!" Alex shouted.

"What?"

"Something's telling me that we need this guy… Stop… We need to pick him up."

"I hope you know what you're doing." Samantha said, pulling the Taurus on to the shoulder of the road.

"Don't worry. I got a good feeling about this." Alex said, rolling down his window and shoving his head out. "Hey, mister, you need a ride?"

"Thank you." Said the mysterious stranger as he opened the back door and climbed in.

"Where you headed?" Alex asked after rolling his window back up and turning in the seat.

"Nowhere in particular; do you mind if I just ride along with you?"

"No problem, you're welcome to stick around as long as you think you need to." Alex responded before anyone could speak up. "What's your name stranger? Mine's Alex, this is Samantha, driving, that there's Bridget beside you. Beside her is my girlfriend, Stephanie."

"KJ…" The stranger replied, "KJ Crow."

Aboard flight 281 from Atlanta to Boston, Sgt. Alan Perkins relaxed in his seat. This was the first time he had been able to relax since Detective Marshall O'Grady had taken command of this case; since he named Alex Rodgers – one of his best friends – the prime suspect of a homicide.

Alan didn't quite understand why O'Grady had such a relentless Rottweiler type hold on Alex being the guy. Alan had known Alex a long time. Although, Alex *was* more than capable of doing such a thing; he wouldn't. Hell, he hadn't even showed up until after the fact anyway. Sure, his fingerprints were found throughout the house, but Stephanie *is* his girlfriend and Alex was over there all the time. Even if Alex *had* killed those men… who in good conscious wouldn't have if they were in that position?

Alan had always had a secret crush on Bridget growing up. Even now, she still knew just the right things to say or do to get to him. He never let her know his true feelings for her though. Because of that, they always had a love/hate relationship. If he had known what was going on inside that house and *had* been the one happening onto it, he wouldn't have hesitated to kill for her.

He supposed he should be grateful that O'Grady sent him instead of going himself. After all, Alan knew Alex better than anyone. If O'Grady had come, he would've just made things worse.

* * *

The plane ride to Boston took longer than he would have liked but then again, Alan hated flying anyway. He had a thirty minute lay over in

Boston before his flight to Bangor began. He was anxious to get there so he could finally have his feet on the ground for longer than thirty minutes.

Deciding to make the best of his layover, he went into one of the diners to get something to eat. Ordering a bacon cheeseburger with the works and some fries, he took a seat at a booth in one corner by a window to eat. Out of the corner of his eye, he caught a flash of reddish-yellow light. At first, he thought it was a flash bulb off a camera but when it came again, he knew exactly what it was; a muzzle flare from most likely a shotgun.

Pulling his sidearm, he moved slowly out of the booth making sure to keep low to the ground and moved toward the door. Soon thereafter, people began running through the hallway just as Alan hit the doorway.

Rounding the corner, heading toward the diner, the flare became brighter, telling him that the person issuing that flare was heading toward him. With each *BLAM BLAM* that came nearer and nearer toward him, it brought with it debris from the walls on either side as the rounds shattered the plaster and drywall into several pieces.

Motioning for the remaining customers and employees, who were now standing in awe of the commotion, to get down, Alan cautiously left the diner and hugged the wall. The man firing the shotgun soon made his appearance, turning with the shotgun as he fired, making sure that he encircled himself with shotgun blasts. His back was to Alan when he emerged from the corridor and as he wheeled around to continue firing, the thunder stopped. He was out of ammunition.

Grabbing some shells from a pocket in the jacket he had on, the gunman started reloading as Alan took aim.

"Police! Drop the weapon, now!" Alan said, aiming his weapon at the man wielding the shotgun. "I said drop it punk… now!"

Instead of following Alan's simple instructions, the stranger slammed the chamber shut and turned his weapon on Alan. With no other alternative, Alan fired three rounds into the stranger, cutting him down where he stood. The shotgun fell to the floor beside him. Quickly moving over to the man, Alan kicked the weapon away from the body and knelt down to ensure that he was dead.

* * *

With the final paperwork out of the way, questions answered, and his own department getting a copy of his report of the events taken place, Alan caught a ride with a local patrolman back to the airport.

Luckily for him, due to the incident, the FAA had grounded all the flights until everything was taken care of. It was just going to take a little longer to get to Bangor than he had hoped.

Alan boarded his flight knowing in just a few minutes the flights would be able to continue as normal. As the flight attendant came around, he asked for a pillow and blanket. He figured he might as well catch a nap while he could.

* * *

On the ground, the door of the airplane opened and the flight attendants were instructing people to slowly exit the plane. Alan got up from his seat, zigzagged through people getting their luggage down, and exited the plane number nine.

Entering the terminal, he located the nearest pay phone and after looking at his watch to find it was now two o'clock, he dialed O'Grady's number using the *collect* option. In three rings, he was rewarded with the detective's voice on the line. Alan waited as the operator asked if he would accept the charges. When his voice came on the line a couple of seconds later, the first thing he asked was why he had called collect.

"Well, sir, you said the flight was on the department so I figured that the call ought to be too."

"Well, what the hell took so long?"

"Did you get my fax from Boston?"

"Yeah, you're not there to gun down some shotgun wielding idiot in an airport. You're there to find Alex Rodgers and bring him back!"

Infuriated, Alan said, "Alright *Lieutenant*, you may outrank me and have seniority in the detective field but I've had about enough of your attitude toward me. I'm doing my job. Against my better judgment, I flew up here on *your* orders to find someone I believe to be innocent of a crime you're dead set on planting on him, just because he showed you up. Now, don't get me wrong *Lieutenant*, Alex Rodgers is far from perfect, but I've known him a long time. He's very capable of a lot of things but if he said he didn't do this, I believe him." Alan knew using O'Grady's rank instead of the title he wanted everyone to use when addressing him would piss him off.

"Sergeant, you just do your job and for God's sake; don't think!"

"Don't worry Lieutenant, I'll do my job. But don't ever threaten me!" Alan said, slamming the receiver back onto the base of the payphone before O'Grady could say another word.

* * *

It took two phone calls to surrounding hotels to find where Alex had stayed the night and Alan was already in pursuit. When he arrived at the Holiday Inn, he approached the receptionist and identified himself.

"I'm looking for a man that stayed here last night by the name of Alex Rodgers. He might've come in with a couple of ladies." Alan said.

"Yes, they were here. It looks like they checked out around eight this morning."

"Has the room been cleaned yet?"

"One of the rooms has been but the other — it looks like, is in the process or hasn't been called in as cleaned yet." The woman said.

"Where is housekeeping located?" He asked the woman behind the counter.

Given the directions, Alan followed the directions given to him and was soon rewarded with a beautiful young blonde housekeeper, that according to her name tag, was named Deidre.

After showing her his badge, Deidre showed him her cart chart where she kept a list of the rooms, she cleaned each day. Luckily, she had been the one who had cleaned Alex Rodgers's room.

"Did you find anything unusual in the room?" Alan asked.

"No," she said.

"Did you find any papers with phone numbers or addresses on them?"

"Come to think of it, I did find a piece of paper with a phone number on it in there."

"May I have it please?"

"Yeah, I'll be right back, I put it back just in case someone came looking for it."

A couple of minutes later Deidre came back with a piece of paper with the name Clayton Green written on it, an address in Augusta, and a phone number.

"Thank you, Deidre, I appreciate the help. Here's my card with my pager number on it, it's toll free, if you think of anything else you may have seen, heard, or found, please page me."

"Do you know where you're going there in Augusta Detective?" Deidre asked.

"I don't even now how to get to Augusta." Alan said honestly.

"Okay, do you have a map or anything?" Deidre asked.

"No, but I have a notepad. If you could just write down the directions then I should be able to find it okay."

"Alright," Deidre said, taking a pen out of her apron and taking the notepad in hand. A few seconds later, she handed it back.

"There you go. Just follow those directions and you should be able to get to Augusta pretty easy. As for this Clayton Green's office, I don't know where that is. I'm sorry."

"That's alright, I have the number. I should be able to find it once they give me directions when I call them. Thank you, ma'am, you've been a lot of help."

* * *

It was three thirty in the afternoon when Alan walked into the law offices of Clayton Green and Associates. He told the receptionist who he was and that he needed to speak with Clayton Green. She left the room and moments later a tall man appeared.

"I'm Clayton Green, how can I help you officer?"

"Sergeant actually, may we speak in private?"

"Sure; follow me to my office Sergeant." Green said.

Once inside, Green showed Alan to a seat and asked him to sit down.

"I'm looking for Alex Rodgers."

"May I inquire as to why Sergeant…?"

"Perkins… Sgt. Alan Perkins. Yes, you may. I'm from the Atlanta Police Department. Alex is a good friend of mine. His girlfriend and her roommate were involved in a felony gone wrong a couple of days ago."

"Were they a participant in the felony?"

"No, actually they were the victims."

"I don't understand Sergeant… Perkins, is it? Please explain what you're talking about."

"Well, its privy information, and I've already told you too much."

"Well, I am – at the moment – the attorney for Mr. Rodgers and his sister, so I am or should be privy to any information that involves him."

"Did you just say Alex has a sister?" Alan said.

"Yes, I did. Long lost sister to be precise," Green said, "now please Sgt. Perkins, tell me what's going on."

Feeling that he was more of a friend to Alex than a cop, Alan told Clayton Green the truth about everything. He told of Detective Marshall O'Grady's ruthless determination to put Alex behind bars. He concluded his story by telling of him being sent to Maine to find Alex and bring him back for more questioning.

"But between you and me, I have no intention of making Alex go back for a witch-hunt. I just want to let Alex know what's going on and see what he wants to do." Alan said.

"Do you have evidence supporting either Detective O'Grady's claim of Alex's guilt or Alex's claim of innocence?" Green asked.

"No, just his word either way. The only evidence O'Grady has fingerprints that could've been there for days, weeks, or even months. As far as I can tell, O'Grady isn't even looking at anyone else."

"Does Alex have an alibi?"

"He says he was in route from his place to hers; he just pulled up shortly after the ambulance left with the girls, taking them to the nearest hospital for observation. O'Grady was all over Alex when we got to the hospital ourselves, simply because Alex got a little smart mouth with him. The following day, O'Grady had him in his office grilling him some more. When Alex asked if he was under arrest for something, O'Grady told him he wasn't."

"Sounds like Alex *is* pretty well covered by the law. I f I have to, I'll go back with Alex and defend him myself. But why are you disobeying your superior?"

"Well, because I believe O'Grady's wrong about Alex. He's going about this entire case all-wrong. He's not investigating any other angles; just Alex."

"Do you believe Alex to be innocent of the charges?"

"I've known Alex a long time and although he is capable of doing such a thing and probably would've, had he gotten there any earlier; I just don't think he did it. We questioned everyone in the neighborhood and no one saw his vehicle anywhere near the scene prior to us arriving on the scene. So, I do believe Alex *is* innocent. I'd stake my badge on it."

"Fair enough," Green said as he began to briefly explain where Alex was going and why. Due to attorney/client confidentiality, he couldn't let Alan know about the money that Alex had inherited but did tell him of the house that was left to him and his sister known as *The Brunswick House.*

In his rental car, Alan pulled out of the parking lot of the law firm and back onto the street. With detailed directions in hand, Alan began making his way toward Highway 17.

At two o'clock, Samantha pulled the Taurus and its five passengers into the town of Rockland. Rockland was a pretty good size town with a range of stores and restaurants – both fast food and sit-in – along Route 1. The town was lined along the Atlantic coast .As they drove along the coastal highway, they could see several boats in the harbor off to the right.

As they drive out of town, they passed a Wal-Mart store, a few more restaurants, and several other residential homes. After passing through the first set of lights, Samantha noticed that the gas tank was coming up on empty .Luckily for her, a gas station/convenience store sat to the left of the next light.

Pulling in along side the pumps of a gas island, Samantha put the car in PARK and got out to pump gas into the rental car while the others remained inside.At the station next to her, a woman pumping gas into her little Volkswagen bug smiled at her when Samantha looked in her direction. Thinking that maybe the woman might be able to answer a few questions for her on directions, Samantha said, "Could I get some directions from you?"

"Sure." The woman said, taking the piece of paper from Samantha .The paper held the directions in which Melissa had given her at Clayton Green's law firm to the house.

"This looks like the address to the old Brunswick house." The woman said, looking at the piece of paper.

"It is. Can you help us find it?"

"Oh no, I don't go up there. It's haunted." The woman said, whispering as she passed the paper back.

"Bah." Samantha retorted.

"You'd be wise to heed my warnin', Miss. If you insist on going there, I'll tell you the way, but you should watch yourself in that house."

"I'm not afraid, ma'am. I appreciate your concern though. I've got plenty of company to help watch my back in there as you can see." Samantha said, waving her hand toward the passengers in her car.

Peering into the window, glancing quickly at the passengers within, the woman looked back toward Samantha. "May I ask why you'd be going to that place?"

"My brother and I inherited the house from our grandfather, Shane Stevenson. We're going up to see what we should do with it."

"Would you like my suggestion Miss?"

"I bet you'd like me to destroy it. Right?"

"Lord, no. My suggestion is simply to close it off. Close it off from everyone. There's a presence in and around that house... a maniacal presence."

"Maniacal?"

"No one has ever been able to identify what this presence might be. Some say it's the evil spirit of the man that murdered the Brunswick's. So, some say, it's the presence of something totally different. Whatever it is... it's evil... pure evil."

As the pump topped the tank of the car and stopped, a single crow flew up and rested on top of the pump. Without removing the nozzle from her gas tank, the woman darted for the building at the sight of the bird. Surprised, Samantha watched as the woman ran into the store. She then looked at the crow that had taken perch atop the pump.

Looking into the rear passenger window, she could see KJ staring back out at her. He mumbled something under his breath, but she couldn't hear what he said. Suddenly, from behind her, the crow cawed and flew away. Replacing the pump handle to where it belonged, Samantha turned toward the store and began walking toward the building. Inside, Samantha found the frightened woman talking with the cashier and telling her all about what had just occurred outside when she gave Samantha directions.

Samantha paid for her fuel, thanked the woman that had given her the advice, and left.

Upon leaving the store, she heard the frightened woman whisper three words that nearly stopped her at the door to ask if she heard her correctly. "Death follows you."

* * *

"What was that all about?" Alex asked as they pulled away from the station.

"What?"

"What was her deal? Why'd she take off like that?"

"She saw a crow."

"So; why would she run off like that?"

Samantha explained what the strange woman had told her about the house and then the last thing she said as Samantha was leaving the store.

"Death follows you?" Alex repeated curiously, "What the hell does she mean by that?"

"I don't know. New England superstition I guess." Samantha said.

"One should not reject superstitions so easily. Embrace it into your mind and think of its meaning; you will then understand that it may be a work of warning past down through the years." KJ said from the back seat.

"Who *are* you… Buddha?" Alex asked sarcastically.

"No Alex; just a friend in search of a way to correct a terrible wrong."

"Alright, what's with the riddles?"

"No riddles my friend; just unfulfilled information."

"Huh?"

"I can not say anymore. You allowed me to ride with you because you felt you could trust me. Now, please, do just that; trust me."

* * *

Turning onto a dirt road five miles up the road from the gas station, Samantha drove northwest another quarter mile, around a curved road, and up a hill. A sign along side the road told them when they were in the right place. On the right side of the road, they saw a sign that read **THE BRUNSWICK HOUSE.** Turning off the main road and into the driveway, only to be stopped by a wrought-iron gate, Samantha pulled the car in park and got out.

"Now what?" She said just as Alex was getting out on the passenger side.

"I'll go check it out. There must be a way in." Alex said.

Approaching the gate, Alex found a rusted chain wrapped around the two ends keeping the doors of the gate shut. He could tell by looking at the hinges along either side of the gate that it could be open either direction. Grabbing hold of the gate bars with both hands, Alex shook the gate back and forth.

Nothing.

"The gate's locked. We'll have to go over." Alex called out.

Overhead, clouds began to quickly roll in. They covered the sun and darkness soon overtook the sky once more. The air around them grew musky with the smell of rain in the horizon and on its way to them, as Alex came back to the car and opened his door to peer inside.

"It's gonna start raining soon. We need to get up to the house now or wait until tomorrow." Alex said. "I think the car'll be fine down here; we can head up to the house on foot."

As the rear doors opened and KJ stepped out from the passenger side, Alex said, "You know, you don't have to stay with us, you can go on your way if you want or I can take you somewhere in particular."

"No, if it's all the same to you, I'd like to stick around and help where I can." KJ said.

"Fair enough; you're welcome to stay. It'll be nice to have another guy around. To tell you the truth, I was starting to feel a little outnumbered." Alex said.

* * *

Upon retrieving their luggage from the trunk of the car and climbing over the gate, they each began hiking the remaining bit of road that was now muddying under foot. The wind began to pick up and forced the trees around them to sway back and forth. The rain soon began to bombard the branches and trunks of the trees, not to mention each of them, with a flurry of stinging wet bullets. Strangely, though, the only one not effected by the rain – in fact, it looked as though he wasn't even being hit by a single drop – was KJ.

A flock of crows perched in the trees above them began to caw in unison as they watched them make their way up the path. Alex thought it peculiar that the birds would remain perched in the trees even as the rain pelted them, but KJ looked up at them and turned his head this way and that, listening to their caws as though he knew exactly what they were saying.

"Death is coming," he said.

Pulling into a full-service fueling station within only minutes from leaving Clayton Green's law office, Alan pulled in and rolled his window down. An attendant quickly made his way over to the window and lowered his head down to greet him.

"What'll it be?"

"Fill her up." Alan said.

"Check your oil?"

"Sure." Alan said as he popped the hood of his rental car. Knowing most rental cars, it probably needed it.

Getting out of the car and going inside, he was greeted again by a man behind the counter. Alan returned his greeting and went to the back to get a soda and a snack. When he was satisfied with his purchases, he returned to his car and paid the attendant that had pumped his gas.

* * *

On the road once more, he rounded through one rotary and followed the road across a bridge. He came to a second rotary and, following directions given to him at Clayton Green's office; followed it to the right. At the first light he came to, he turned left and found himself on Highway 17 just as the directions said he would. He was twenty minutes outside of Augusta when it began to rain furiously.

"Well, this sucks. I thought Maine was called the Vacation State." Alan said to himself.

Thunder cracked across the sky as the wind picked up speed and strength. Rain plummeted from the clouds above with an unbelievable force. The windshield wipers of Alan's rental car – even at high speed – were barely a match for the water hitting the car.

"That's it, I'm pulling over." Alan said frustrated, pulling the car onto the shoulder of the road.

Just then, his pager went off. Looking at the numerical message, Alan found it to be Detective O'Grady. "Damn! What the hell does he want now?" Alan said angrily into the car.

CHAPTER 18

With rain crashing down hard from overhead, they hurried up the quickly muddying road as fast as they could. As lightning clashed across the sky, their destination was illuminated… the Brunswick House.

Standing two and a half stories high from ground to rooftop, the house looked as sinister as Clayton Green tried to impose when telling the story of it. A horseshoe shaped porch enveloped the front of the house, a single set of steps set in front of the porch leading from the ground up to a solid oak front door. Among the trees surrounding the property, perched several more crows cawing in unison.

The house that had been haunting Samantha's dreams every night for over the past week was standing completely tangible before her. As the others made their way to the front steps in order to ascend them, Samantha remained frozen in place with a frightened stare in her eyes.

As Alex began to ascend the steps, he looked back to see that his sister was not moving. Quickly moving away from the steps and to her side, he waved his hand in front of her face, he said, "Samantha… Earth calling Samantha… You okay?"

After several minutes of staring at the house, not saying anything at all, not responding to anything Alex was trying to say to her, she finally turned her head toward him and said, "I can't go in there."

"Why not?"

"I just can't. You can have the house; I don't want any part of it."

"What? Hey, what's going on?"

"I've dreamt of this house Alex." Samantha said, turning to face her brother but keeping her voice low so as to not alert the others who were now standing at the door staring at them.

"I've seen evil things in this house. I can't go in there. I won't go in!" She said, turning and starting to make her way back down the hill to the car. Alex grabbed her by the arm gently and stopped her.

"Sam, look, I don't even know if I want this house yet. Those dreams were just that… dreams. Don't let them rule your life. You said yourself, remember, you don't run away from anything. If this place *is* haunted, let's find out together. Come with us Sam… please."

Samantha stood with her head bowed down. "I'm scared Alex. I've never been this scared. Ever since Dan died, life just hasn't been the same for me and now the nightmare I've been having of this house… it's become a reality. I'm afraid of what may lay in store for us inside."

"We're all scared Sam; it's what you do with that fear that determines what's going to happen to you. If we stick together, we'll be okay."

Reluctantly, Samantha looked at her brother and said, "You're right. You're absolutely right."

Returning to the group, she went to the front door and turned the knob. With squeaks and stiffness, the door slowly opened revealing a huge foyer inside the door.

Standing inside the foyer, they each stood in amazement at the sight of how huge the inside of the house looked compared to the outside. There was an entrance to what looked like a dining room to the left; to the right was a stairwell and another entrance to what looked like a living room setting. Passed the stairwell, further in, was a hallway leading toward the back of the house.

"Alright, we should check this place out. So, let's split up like this. . ."

"Wait a minute, Alex; you said we would stick together." Samantha said.

"We will, but we'll get more of a layout of the house if we split into two teams and search the house completely to get a better feel for it."

"I don't think this is a good idea, Alex." Stephanie said.

"It'll be fine. Please, just trust me. Okay, this is how I want to do this; KJ, you go with Samantha and take the downstairs. I'll take Stephanie and Bridget and search upstairs.

"We'll meet back here in the foyer in half an hour, regardless of how much ground we've covered." Alex said.

* * *

"Look at the stains on these steps Alex." Stephanie said as they ascended the staircase.

"Looks like blood."Bridget said.

"It must've been too difficult to get up when they redid the house." Alex noted.

"You'd think someone would've covered it up with a carpet or something." Stephanie said.

"I'm sure it's been tried." Alex said, pointing down at the floor in front of the steps. "Look at the edges of the steps there. There's carpet fragments snagged on that nail."

"You're right; someone did try covering it up. But who would rip up the carpeting?" Bridget said.

At the top of the stairs lay a larger stain on the hard wood floor where it appeared carpet had once been also. "This is really spooky." Stephanie said, grasping Alex's arm.

"No need to be scared, there's no one else here but us." Alex reassured her.

* * *

Walking through the dining room into the kitchen, Samantha stood in amazement at the mere size of the kitchen.

"I don't think I've ever seen a kitchen this big outside of a four-star restaurant," she said.

"Smells as though someone's been cooking in here," KJ said. "Smells like a stew of some kind. Do you smell that?"

"Faintly," Samantha said, smelling the air.

"Seems like good ol' Grandpa made sure to equip the kitchen… "Samantha said.

"Only one problem," KJ said, flipping a switch on the wall. "No electricity."

"There's got to be a utility box around here somewhere." Samantha said.

"Let's go downstairs and check it out." KJ said.

"I'm not going down there without a light." Samantha said sternly.

"I'm sure there will be a power switch down there to bring the power back on in the house." KJ said. "And besides, I don't think you want to stay up here alone."

Quickly contemplating the scenario in her mind, she agreed to follow him down the stairs.

* * *

Stepping into the first room they came to, Alex found it to be a bedroom. It was fully furnished and had surprisingly little dust or cobwebs. "My grandpa must have made sure that we were comfortable," Alex said.

Suddenly the lights in the bedroom and hallway lit up nearly blinding them.

"I'd say Samantha and our new friend have found the breaker box." Alex said, rubbing his eyes.

"I'd say so." Bridget remarked sarcastically.

"Look at this bedroom; it looks like someone lived here not too long ago."Stephanie said.

"My grandfather did; Clayton Green told us that he was doing some extensive repairs on the house before he died." Alex said.

"Can't tell it by the outside of this place, but you sure can by the inside," Bridget said, walking back out into the hallway. "I'm gonna check more rooms now that we have some light."

* * *

Returning to the kitchen almost in a sprint, Samantha stopped and drew deep breaths. KJ arrived at her side shortly after, "It's very cold down there. I think it wise if we all remain topside." KJ said.

"I'll second that. I'm sorry I panicked down there. That's not like me; I'm usually solid as a rock." Samantha said.

"No need for apologies Samantha, you have been through a lot in the past week."

"Yeah, I guess you're right." Samantha agreed then as though she were slapped across the face, she looked into the eyes of this dark stranger as a thought occurred to her.

"Wait a minute, how do you know what I've been through over the past week? I've never seen you before this afternoon."

"One does not have to be part of the show in order to know what had happened before he began watching… or to know what may come in the future." KJ replied.

"What?"

"The answers to all of your questions will be revealed in time. Just know; I am on your side and I am here to make right what went wrong."

"Okay. You're a very confusing man Mr. Crow." Samantha stated.

"Please… call me KJ."

"Okay KJ; now that we have light, why don't we finish this search?"

"Lead the way my friend." KJ replied.

* * *

"Alex! Stephanie! Come quick!" Bridget hollered from the hallway.

Following her voice, Alex and Stephanie found Bridget in the room opposite the master bedroom in which they had been in.

"What is it?" Alex said, coming into the room.

"Look on the wall… on the other side of the bed." Bridget said, pointing her finger where she wanted Alex to look.

On the wall, in what appeared to be dried blood, were two words clearly indicating that they were not welcome by someone; *GET OUT!* "What the hell?" Alex said, approaching the bloody letters.

The closer he approached; however, the words and the blood began to slowly fade. When he reached the wall, the image had completely vanished.

"What the hell?" Alex repeated.

"Did you see anything else in any of the other rooms?"

"No, other than they were all furnished just like this one. I thought you said your grandfather was the last to live here." Bridget answered.

"He was. I don't understand any of this. Let's go back downstairs and meet up with Samantha and KJ." Alex said, leading the way out of the bedroom.

"I don't like this, Alex. I'm scared." Stephanie said.

"I know sweetie, but as long as you're with me, you'll be alright. I promise."

* * *

Across the main hall and past the stairwell, Samantha and KJ walked into the adjoining room and found it to be the living room. It too was fully furnished with a long couch approximately six feet long, a recliner, a coffee table set perfectly center to the couch, and a console television sat against the wall. A VCR set atop television and a four-and-a-half-foot standing lamp beside it. A love seat set against the opposite wall under a window and was positioned somewhat of a greater distance from the other pieces of furniture.

A door stood at the corner of the room on the same wall as the TV. Walking through this door, Samantha found herself in a library of some kind. KJ walked closely behind as she ventured further inside.

"You are or were at one time a police officer. Am I correct in my assumption Samantha?" KJ said, watching her movements.

"Yes, I'm a detective with the Tulsa P. D. in Oklahoma. Why do you ask?"

"Your motions as we move through these rooms have become more fluid. That can mean that you were once, or are currently, a police officer or soldier. That type of movement comes with years of training."

"Very perceptive, but I'm seriously considering a new career choice."

"Your true path awaits you; you have merely to continue traveling until you reach it. When you find it… you will know."

"You know what, I must be losing it."

"Why do you say that?"

"You're starting to make sense."

"All things come with time Samantha."

"Yeah right," Samantha said as she walked through the small library. "There's got to be a million books here. There are shelves on every wall, and everyone is full."

From the main hall, they heard a banging sound that sounded like someone knocking on the front door. They quickly made there way back to the foyer to investigate, but when they arrived; it stopped. From the direction of the stairs, Samantha heard the others joining them.

"Did you guys hear that?" Samantha asked as they joined her and KJ at the front door.

"Hear what?" Stephanie said.

"That banging; did any of you hear it?"

"No, I didn't." Alex said

"We didn't either," Stephanie said, answering for Bridget as well.

"I don't see how you couldn't. It was loud. KJ and I heard it all the way on the other side of the house."

"Well, we didn't hear any banging. Did you find anything interesting?" Alex asked.

"Depends on what you mean by interesting." Samantha said.

"Anything, well… weird… out of the ordinary."

"Yeah, the kitchen has a very strong aroma to it, like someone just finished cooking a stew or something." Samantha said.

"Everything seems to be neat and orderly around here, hardly any dust or cob webs. Surely a man with ailments like your grandfather couldn't have kept this place this clean." Bridget said.

"You're right, that does seem awfully strange." Stephanie agreed.

"Well, Sam, what do you want to do? It's getting kind of late. It seems that all the bedrooms are furnished, and it's gonna take a couple of days to really come up with a plan of action on what to do with this place." Alex said, looking at his sister.

"Are you suggesting we stay the night here?" Samantha asked.

"Well… yes. As long as we're all here together, I think we can deal with whatever happens."

"I really don't like the idea but I don't think the weather's gonna let up. There's nothing in the kitchen to cook for dinner though." Samantha said.

"We'll figure something out. It's still early."

"What about the car?" Bridget asked.

"Well, nothing can bother it down there; it's off the main road so it can't be hit by oncoming traffic or anything. It's fine where it's at. As for food, we can always go to the store if we need to." Alex said.

"Well, we each might as well find a bedroom to bunk down for the night then go from there." Samantha said reluctantly.

Passing a fork in the road leading to Highway 32, Alan noticed a car swerving not too far ahead of him.

"What the hell?"

Suddenly the car began to spin out of control, slamming hard against a guardrail, whipping the car around once, twice, and then a third and final time; it came to a stop down a steep embankment.

"Oh shit!" He shouted aloud.

Quickly braking and pulling on to the shoulder of the road, Alan got out of the car and stood at the edge of the road peering down toward the car.

"Hello…! Is everyone all right down there?" Alan shouted. When no answer came, he quickly made his way down the embankment to see if the person or persons within the car were okay.

Alan repeated his questions as he drew nearer.

Still no answer.

Approaching the driver's side window, he noticed some movement inside. "Hello," Alan shouted once more, "Is everyone okay in there?"

This time, a muffled moan came from the front seats. A second later, another noise sounded from inside the car that nearly stopped his heart in mid-beat. A low but distinguished whimper that could have only come from a baby called out to him.

As nature's waterworks finally started to let up a little, Alan quickly took advantage and tried to open the door. The low whimper grew louder and louder into a full out wail as Alan worked on the door. It sounded to Alan that the child might be hurt. At the sound of the child in danger, a sudden burst of adrenaline gave Alan super human strength. Alan pulled on the crumpled door as hard as he could for several tugs until it finally gave.

With the door open, Alan reached into the car to find a man behind the steering wheel. Putting two fingers against the man's carotid artery, Alan felt for a pulse and found a faint and extremely weak one. A woman lay in the passenger seat, her belt barely hanging off of her, as she was reaching behind her toward the baby seat in the back.

Looking past the father in the driver's seat, Alan could see the baby carrier still strapped in the seat behind them. Suddenly the car grew quiet. The whimpering that had brought him the strength to yank open the door fell silent. Realizing that something was definitely wrong, Alan reached into the car, looking for the seatbelt release so he could safely remove the father from his seat and found it almost immediately.

Pulling the man from his seat, Alan laid him on the ground outside the car and then quickly poked his head inside once more to get a better look into the back seat. A blanket lay over the carrier in the back, most likely to shield the baby's young eyes from the sun as they drove; even though it had been raining.

Lifting the blanket, the baby beneath began to cry once more. Alan's breath came back to him all at once as he let out a gasp. He hadn't even realized he had been holding it until then. He felt much better upon hearing the baby's cry.

hoosing the master bedroom for their own, Alex and Stephanie decided that their new property needed to be properly consummated. With the door shut behind them, Alex entered her with slow purposeful intent, feeling her shutter beneath him with each thrust and gyration of his hips. She matched his movements with her own body, bringing each of them equal amounts of pleasure.

After ten minutes in the missionary position, they changed positions; this time with Stephanie on top, rocking and gyrating her hips atop him until they came together in a mutual climax.

Stephanie tried not to make much sound, and for the most part succeeded, until that very moment of climax when she could no longer hold it in. With a scream of pleasure, she collapsed atop Alex exhausted and satisfied.

Wrapping his arms around her and holding close to his chest, Alex had the feeling that everything was finally going to be okay. When she finally sat up, she straddled him for a moment, then dismounted him as if he were a horse, she had just finished riding for her amusement. She laid down against him on his right side, still with one hand draped across his chest, and lay her head on his shoulder.

* * *

Bridget volunteered to go back to town in order to pick up some groceries so that they could eat dinner before retiring for the night.

"I will accompany you, Bridget. Food is the energy in which the soul needs to boost its awareness. It helps to hone the psyche to strengthen the mind." KJ said.

"Okay…," Bridget said not quite sure what to think of that statement. She just hoped that he didn't start calling her *'Grasshopper'* like the monks did in those old Kung Fu shows.

* * *

As the door shut behind Bridget and KJ, Samantha decided that she should do something to occupy her time now that she was the only one left downstairs. She knew why Alex and Stephanie went upstairs so quickly after they had all decided to stay the night. She couldn't blame them really. They were cute together.

Feeling a little more confident now that the power was on and she could see where she was going, she retrieved her gun from her bag and began to continue her search of the house. She was very interested to see what had drawn her grandfather to purchase this house. What was so special about it?

"Don't look too deep Kid." A voice said from behind her.

Wheeling around on her heel simultaneously drawing her pistol from its holster attached now to her belt, she took aim in the direction behind her only to find…

Nothing. There was nothing there. Keeping the gun unsheathed, she held it at the ready pointed down at her side; she continued to search the hallway beside the staircase.

The voice that warned her not to look too deep was unmistakably that of Dan Riley. In fact, she was certain that all the times she had heard someone speaking to her from behind, it had been Dan. She knew that the apparitions that she had seen on the plane were also that of Dan. She knew all of this; she knew the whole time… she just didn't want to admit it to herself until now.

Now, though it was undeniable, unmistakable, and unexplainable; it *was* Dan. Somehow, he was trying to give her a message. The question was… what was it?

B efore Alex and Stephanie had departed for their little adventure upstairs, Bridget had made sure to collect some spending cash from him so she could do the grocery shopping. Now, in the rental car and behind the wheel, she started the engine and pulled back onto the dirt road. Within a few minutes, she was back on Route 1 heading back into town.

"If I remember correctly, there were a couple of grocery stores we passed back there in town. Which one should we go to?" Bridget said, quickly glancing over to her silent and mysterious passenger.

"I would prefer to stop at the convenience store that we stopped at earlier," KJ said.

"Why? They're not going to have much of a selection."

"One does not need a wide selection to know what he wants to eat. The items at that store will suffice us for the night." KJ said.

"Okay, whatever."

Pulling into the parking lot of the convenience store nearly five minutes later, they parked in the parking spaces provided and got out of the car. When Bridget turned to look across the roof of the car, she found that her mysterious new friend had not joined her outside the confines of the car. Peering back inside the car, she said, "Aren't you coming in?"

"No, I will remain outside until you return. If you need me, I will know." KJ said.

"You are one weird dude." Bridget said, closing the driver's side door and heading into the store.

* * *

The rain had subsided but it seemed to grow darker than normal outside. Bridget had been inside the store only a few minutes when KJ noticed the three crows perched atop the store's marquee.

Getting out of the car, he made his way to the front glass doors. Inside, just before he stepped up to the door, he noticed three armed men holding weapons and wearing ski masks. The customers were all face down on the floor.

Standing to one side of the door, he peered inside to find the best opportune moment to get inside. Finding that the man nearest the door was looking from left to right, not really giving him more than a second at a time of opportunity, he realized that he wasn't going to get a better chance. Opening the door and stepping inside, KJ stood silently inside the entrance. The man closest to the door noticed him and ordered him to get on the floor. KJ did not respond.

"Get on the floor asshole!" The man shouted again, raising his weapon at the same time.

"There is a better way to do this." KJ said, trying to calm the man.

"Get down on the floor now!" The man demanded again, taking a step closer, motioning with his weapon the direction he wished KJ to go.

"As you wish," KJ said, rolling his eyes upwards while his lids remained open until only the whites of his eyes showed. Raising his arms out to his side with his palms facing the ceiling, he began mumbling under his breath.

"Get on the..." The man shouted one last time as he cocked his weapon and became ready to fire.

Suddenly, the three crows that had been perched atop the roof of the store swooped into the still open door, behind KJ, and dove toward the man with his weapon trained on him. Simultaneously dropping his weapon in order to cover his face, the other two gunmen raised their weapons and started to fire at the birds.

As the bullets from their guns exited their muzzles, they missed their intended targets and fell harmlessly to the floor. It was as if there was absolutely no momentum behind each round to carry them any farther than six or seven inches in front of the weapons.

KJ quickly came out of his trance, rolled across the floor, and grabbed the gun that the first man had dropped. Standing back up, he took aim at the closest of the two men and said, "Get on the floor."

Both men did as they were told and KJ went back to the door and opened it, allowing the three crows to exit the same way they had entered. "I told you there was a better way of doing this." KJ said, approaching the first man with the gun trained on him.

Bridget stood up from the floor and watched as KJ put the muzzle of the weapon to the man's temple. "No KJ… don't!" She shouted.

"No worries, Bridget. I am not here to cause death to anyone, only to stop events that would otherwise alter what is to be." KJ said, dropping the weapon to the floor.

When the weapon fell to the floor, the man tried to get up and run out of the store. KJ stopped him, however, with one punch across the bridge of the man's nose. He fell back down against the floor unconscious.

Approaching from behind him, Bridget said, "I don't understand you KJ, but I'm glad you were here."

The clerk that had been on the floor behind the counter came out and threw her arms around KJ's neck thanking him for what he had done. "It was only what needed to be done." KJ said when she let him go.

"You take anything you want from here. It's on me," she said.

"We insist on paying for what we get. Otherwise, we are no different than the men who tried to rob you." KJ replied.

"I insist." The woman said.

"Very well… Your generosity will be rewarded ten-fold." He said as he and Bridget began making rounds throughout the store, getting things that they might need for themselves and the others back at the house.

* * *

In the car, with the rain beating down atop the roof, Bridget told KJ the story of how she, Stephanie, and Alex had started this little adventure. She told him of the incident at her house and how scared she had been. Tears rolled down her cheeks as she spoke of the ordeal.

When she was finished, she waited quietly for KJ response. After a few minutes, he gave it…

"Sounds as though you have been through a great deal. I saw something in your eyes back at the store that told me that something was wrong. The eyes, you know, are the windows to the soul. Each pair tells a unique story; all it takes is someone to take the time to read them. For the ones that are pure in heart, it is not difficult for them to see the story and be patient enough to wait for it to be told." KJ said.

"You're not going to tell anyone about what I told you, are you? Cause if you did, Alex could get into some real trouble." Bridget said.

"Mine is to listen and not to judge. Nor do I repeat what I hear. Alex did right by helping you, even if the police think differently. I have a feeling that there is one, however, that believes in Alex and will help him when the moment is right."

"You must mean Alan." Bridget said. "But how would you know about Alan?"

"Your heart speaks of him."

"I didn't say his name. What do you mean 'my heart speaks of him'?"

"You stated that a Sgt. Perkins had been the first to arrive at the scene. When you spoke his name, your eyes shimmered. When you spoke his first name to me a moment ago, they shimmered again… as if they were smiling."

"Man, you're one crazy guy. I *was* meaning to ask you something though." Bridget said.

"And what is that my new friend?"

"Back at the store… how did you control those birds?"

Their conversation ended when they arrived at the gate leading up the driveway once more. "I will tell you all when the time is right. This, I promise you." KJ said as he got out of the car and went to the gate.

"It's locked… remember?"

"Momentarily locked," KJ said as he stood in front of the lock to the gate shielding Bridget with his back so that she could not see what he was doing. He spoke softly to where she couldn't hear and then stepped back away from the gate as the doors swung open.

"How'd you do that?" Bridget said as KJ climbed back inside the car.

"All will be revealed in time."

"When the hell will that be?"

"I told you. . . when the time is right." KJ said as they drove past the gate and up the driveway.

"So, when will the time be right?" Bridget persisted.

"Soon."

Flipping the driver's seat up by way of the lever beside the seat, Alan reached in the back and carefully unfastened the safety belt that was holding the baby carrier in place. Grabbing the handle of the carrier and slowly pulling it out of the car, Alan looked down to see a baby girl peering back at him. At the sight of him, her tears subsided and she began to calm.

From the edge of the road above him, he heard someone call out, "Is everything all right down there?"

Looking up, Alan noticed a man standing on the shoulder with a flashlight pointed down at him. He hadn't even realized how dark it was in the ravine surrounded by all the trees until now.

"We got some people hurt down here… Call 911!" Alan shouted back.

Putting the baby carrier on the ground beside the father, Alan put the seat back upright and reached across to pull the unconscious mother out from the passenger seat. Just as he was pulling her head out of the car with his arms under hers, he heard the man at the top yell down, "Help's on the way! Is there anything I can do?"

"Yeah, there's a baby down here. Could you come down here and get her? She needs to get out of this weather before it gets any worse."

Making his way down the ravine, the man appeared before Alan in only a few seconds. He was older than he was, maybe forty or so, and had a dark beard and blue eyes. Looking into them, he could tell that this man was kind. He didn't know that many people in his life who owned eyes like that.

Pulling the woman, the rest of the way out of the car just as the Samaritan reached him, Alan laid her beside her husband on the ground and handed the man the baby carrier with the little girl inside.

* * *

God must have been smiling on Alan, for just as the man reached the top of the ravine once again with the baby carrier in hand, the sound of approaching sirens sounded in the distance. How sweet that sound was. Minutes later, a state trooper appeared at the top of the ravine.

"What seems to be the problem?" The trooper yelled down.

"There's been an accident!" Alan shouted back.

The trooper pressed the button on a radio mic that he had attached to his shoulder lapel and spoke directly into it. A second later, he shouted back down, "There's another trooper on his way as well as an ambulance. Do you need assistance yourself?"

"No, I'm fine. I just need some help getting these two-up top." Alan shouted back.

Making his way down the ravine to join him, the trooper barely missed slipping on the muddy terrain and falling flat on his butt, "What's your name sir?" He said, making his way to Alan.

Reaching into his back pocket, Alan fished for his identification while the trooper exercised caution by keeping one hand on the butt of his sidearm. Alan handed his wallet to the trooper. After reading the identification and handing it back to him, the trooper said, "Sgt. Perkins, what can I do?"

"I sent a baby up in her carrier with that man you just passed. I don't think she's injured but I would appreciate it if you made sure she's safe until the ambulance arrives." Alan said.

"I'll make sure she's taken care of." The trooper said.

"These two need to get up top as well. I don't know if it will happen but I wouldn't want them down here by the car if it did catch fire." Alan said.

"I don't think that would be very advisable Sgt. Perkins; just in case these two have injuries themselves, we might hurt them more by moving them. We should let the EMT's handle them. Besides I don't smell any gasoline, do you?" The trooper said.

"No, I don't. You're right. Besides, the mother here looks to have a broken leg and a face laceration. We probably would hurt her more if we moved her." Alan agreed.

* * *

Within a matter of five to ten minutes, another trooper pulled his cruiser behind the first with his lights already on. The trooper started to make his way down the ravine himself but was stopped when the first told him of the baby in the carrier with the Samaritan up top. He decided to stay with the baby. The ambulance arrived shortly after and parked at an angle in the road.

The driver got out and placed road cones fifteen feet to the rear and ten feet to the front of the ambulance. Another cruiser arrived directly behind the ambulance and that trooper began his duty of directing traffic.

The paramedics made their way down the ravine with their gurney and to the location where Alan and the first trooper awaited them. One of the paramedics grabbed her radio and announced that they would need another ambulance immediately after being told that there was a baby up top.

* * *

Within a total of thirty minutes, both the injured adults and the infant were loaded up in both ambulances; the man by himself in one, the mother and her child together in the other. The trooper wrote in detail Alan's statement leading up to his involvement and the actions he took in order to save the family's life.

Once satisfied with his reports, the trooper thanked Alan for his quick thinking and judgment in handling the situation and before getting back into his cruiser, asked Alan why he was in Maine.

"I'm here to find a friend of mine that might be able to help with a murder investigation back in Atlanta. My Lieutenant is quite lazy and figured since this guy was a friend of mine, I might have better luck getting him to come back to help." Alan lied.

"Aren't they all?" The trooper agreed to the laziness of some higher-ranking management. "If there's anything that I might be able to help you with, please don't hesitate to call."

Handing Alan his card, the trooper got behind the wheel of his cruiser and pulled back onto the highway. Almost with exact calculation as Alan entered his own car and shut the door, the rain began falling once again.

The sound of the rain hitting the back patio just outside the dining room imitated a drumbeat beckoning Samantha to answer its call. The sliding glass door, which looked to have been installed within the past year or so, stood against the back wall of the dining room. Samantha opened it as easily as if it were brand new.

A cold shiver raced across her spine. She quickly turned around when she thought she felt something or someone behind her. Nothing was there, however, but she had that deep gut feeling that she *was* being watched. Turning once more to the patio outside, she started to take a step onto the hard wood floor when she felt something touch her shoulder.

Turning quickly once more, she was disappointed to find only what appeared to be a lightning bug loose in the dining room. The flicker of light emanating from it quickly disappeared as she watched it soar across the room. Realizing that she must be imagining things, she turned once more to the patio and watched as the rain continued its merciless hypnotic beat against the hard wood.

Stepping onto the floor of the patio, Samantha felt the cold mist of the rain and wind combined as it sprayed gently across her face. The rain quickly soaked her head as she continued outside forcing her hair to mat against her scalp.

With a sudden sharp pain to her temple followed quickly by a flash of lightning, the darkness gave way to the image of a man stumbling through the backyard. Peering into the night, trying to get a better look at the man, Samantha could see that he was trying desperately to walk into the back woods. He was holding his right arm limp at his side and his neck with his left hand. He was stumbling and swaying as though he were in a great amount of pain. Starting to take a step off the patio to follow him, the man suddenly vanished just as quickly as it had appeared.

Stepping into the not too recently manicured back lawn, even as she was being pummeled hard by the rain, she saw something gleaming in the grass only a few feet away from the edge of the patio.

Reaching down into the tall blades of grass, she retrieved a rusted and tainted looking hunting knife with at least a seven-inch blade. It looked to be quite old and had been there for some time. How someone could have missed it over the years while keeping the landscape up, she couldn't figure out.

Pulling a cloth handkerchief from her jacket pocket, she wrapped the knife inside and brought it back into the house. Shutting the door behind her, she took a seat at the table.

Carefully unfolding the handkerchief, Samantha examined the knife carefully and found clumps of dark rust, or mud, or something else altogether stuck to the blade. She figured that over time, whatever it had been on the knife, had dried and literally bonded to the blade. Wrapping the knife once more, she put the weapon back inside her jacket pocket and went to get Alex.

* * *

"Well, it looks like KJ and Bridget are back." Alex said as he rose from the bed, putting his jeans on.

"You hungry?" He said, turning to Stephanie who was now hugging Alex's pillow against her bare breasts.

"You go on ahead. I'm tired. I'm gonna take a nap. Would you come and get me when supper's ready?"

"You sure?" He asked unsure of leaving her alone.

"Go… I'll be fine. Just come get me when supper's ready."

"Okay; I'll be up to get you soon." Alex said, pulling his shirt on. He leaned down and kissed her on the lips, then left, shutting the door behind him.

It was almost instantly from the moment she heard the door shut behind him when sleep overtook Stephanie. With the events of the past few days finally behind her, she was completely exhausted. For the first time since before those events had taken place, her sleep was uninterrupted by nightmares.

Her dream of long faraway fantasies with Alex was interrupted, however, when she heard a man's voice emanating from the hallway just outside her door. She could tell by the sound of his voice that it wasn't Alex and it didn't sound like KJ either. The voice wasn't just talking. Whoever it was; was screaming one solitary word: "*NO!*"

Sitting up in the bed, clutching the very pillow she had stolen from Alex when he got up, to her chest; she pulled the sheets over her naked breasts and listened to the darkness.

The man's scream suddenly fell silent. A moment later, a light erupted into the room as the bedroom door flew open, revealing a man dressed in pair of jeans and a flannel shirt. The man rushed into the room quickly and with urgency in his movement.

Moving toward the bed, the man was suddenly grabbed from behind by another man wearing what looked like a jumpsuit of some kind. The second man literally threw the first across the room where he landed weightlessly across the bed. Stephanie gasped in surprise and a scream caught in her throat when she realized that the man literally didn't weigh anything.

When she looked down at him, he looked up into her eyes and literally evaporated right in front of her eyes. The second man, at this moment, was making his way quickly toward the bed with a wicked looking knife in his hand. Suddenly, he too evaporated into the air as if he were made of steam.

Shaking her head left to right, left to right again in quick successions; she tried to grasp what she had just witnessed when suddenly, just as mysteriously as they had disappeared, they reappeared. This time, however, the man with the knife was standing over the bed. When the man sprawled across the bed began pushing himself up, the man with the knife plunged it into his side. This time, the scream did not stick in her throat and she let it out with all she was worth.

* * *

Bridget and KJ had just arrived safely inside the house soaking wet with a handful of groceries between them when they heard a scream coming from upstairs. Alex was holding the door open for them but quickly abandoned his post when he heard Stephanie's scream.

When he reached the staircase, he was stopped dead in his tracks when he spotted a pool of blood quickly forming at the base of the stairs. Thinking that something had happened to Stephanie, he hollered out her name as he began climbing the stairs two at a time.

At the head of the stairs, he was stopped once again in his tracks when he found the source of the pool of blood at the bottom of the stairs. A woman lay covered in blood on the floor just at the top of the staircase. She had been ripped open in a most vicious fashion. Although he wanted to look away, Alex was transfixed to her eyes which stared blindly into his.

The feeling of an elbow being jammed into his rib cage knocked him out of his brief hypnosis. Blinking his eyes and looking in the direction the elbow had come, he found Samantha by his side.

"You okay?" she said.

Suddenly Stephanie's screams became audible to him once again and he didn't even bother answering her question. He quickly rushed through the open door to the master bedroom.

Stephanie was sitting up in the bed holding a sheet and a pillow to her chest. He went to her and pulled her close to him, holding her as he tried to calm her.

"What happened?" He finally asked as Stephanie finally quit screaming and calmed down enough to talk.

Stephanie began telling him what she saw when she noticed that Samantha, Bridget, and their mysterious new friend were standing at the doorway. Embarrassed, she stopped her story and asked if she could get dressed and tell the rest of the story downstairs and away from this room.

* * *

Ten minutes after they had returned downstairs, put up the groceries, and sat around the huge dining room table that Shane Stevenson had left for them inside the huge dining room; Stephanie concluded her story right up to the point to where Alex had arrived inside the room.

When the story was completed and they began discussing what she could have seen, KJ stood up from the table and told them that they all needed food in order to think more clearly. They didn't bother to understand him; they just allowed him to make the supper and continued with their conversation.

"Well, I have an interesting tale of my own." Samantha said, pulling a cloth handkerchief from her jacket pocket and putting it on the table. It looked as if it had something in it. When she opened it, she revealed a tattered and rusted looking knife.

With a shrill of fear escaping Stephanie's lips even as she was pushing her chair away from the table, she brought her hands to her mouth trying to muffle the screams as she stared at the knife.

"What's wrong?" Alex said, getting up from his seat beside her and kneeling down at her side.

"That's the knife… that's the knife." She said, pointing at the knife in the handkerchief.

"What do you mean?" Alex said.

"That's the knife that stabbed that man."

"The man you saw upstairs?"

"Yes… that's the knife."

Returning his attention to the knife sitting on the table, Alex could see that it was fairly old, rusted, with a lot of discoloration on the blade. The blade was about seven inches long from tip to hilt. It resembled that of a hunting knife about twenty to maybe twenty-five years old.

"Where did you find this?" Alex asked, examining the weapon.

"I was actually going to show you this earlier Alex." Samantha said, looking over to him.

"Where did you find it?" He repeated.

"That makes for an interesting story like I told you." She said as she began explaining the circumstances leading to her finding the knife in the backyard.

"I feel like something's out there." She said getting up from her seat and walking to the sliding glass door in which she had went out of earlier when she found the knife. "Something evil."

"You may be imagining things," Alex said, "but then again. . . I saw something on the staircase that I wish to God I hadn't."

"What?" Stephanie said as she finally calmed down and grabbed Alex by the hand.

"Well, when I was heading up the stairs earlier, I saw a pool of blood at the base of the stairs. When I got to the top, I saw… I saw…"

"What did you see?" Bridget asked with interest. She had been following closely behind Alex and Samantha went they went up the stairs and had seen him freeze at the top but didn't know why.

"I saw a woman… naked… bloody… just completely torn apart." Alex said, grimacing at the mere thought of what he had seen.

"I think I've seen that myself." Samantha said, returning to the table but not to any chair.

"You saw her? You mean I'm *not* just seeing things?" Alex said.

"Oh no, you're seeing things alright." Samantha said seriously. "I think we all are."

"What do you mean?" Bridget asked.

"I mean, we're all-seeing things. Alone or together, we're all seeing them. I saw that same murdered woman on the floor up there, but not when you did. That was part of my reoccurring dreams – or I should say nightmares – over the past couple of weeks but more so in the past few days. Lately, however, I've been seeing things while totally awake. I didn't want to say anything, but now I don't feel I have a choice. Almost immediately following the death of Dan… I've been seeing him everywhere."

"Your partner… you've been seeing your partner?" Alex said, trying to understand.

"Yes, I've been seeing Dan a lot. I think he's trying to help me find my way… the right path to choose, so to speak. It's hard to explain but. . . " She said as she now fell silent trying to pull herself together.

"The spirits of the dead are restless in this house." KJ said, stepping into the dining room with two platters in hand. One with sandwiches and the other was a bowl full of chips.

Completely hushed by his statement, everyone looked at him in bewilderment as he entered the room and placed the items on the table in front of Alex and Stephanie.

"My earlier statement holds truer now. Death is coming." KJ said. "However, I believe the statement should change to. . . death is here."

"Something happen to you KJ?" Alex asked.

"Let me answer that." Bridget said.

As they each took a sandwich from the plate in front of them, Bridget began to set the scene of an incredible, almost unbelievable story.

* * *

With stomachs full of sandwiches and minds full of an extravagant tale, they all looked at KJ in unison with wonder and awe after hearing of the unbelievable actions that he had taken inside the store.

"All right, now it's time to talk KJ." Bridget ordered when she finished her story.

KJ started to protest but was interrupted by a knock at the front door.

According to Alan's watch, it was nearly six o'clock in the evening when he pulled his rental car into the town of Rockland where, according to Clayton Green, was only five to ten miles from the location of the house in which Alex Rodgers and his sister had inherited.

"What's going on here?" Alan said, pulling into a small convenience store.

Within minutes after entering the store, Alan could see immediately that something big had happened. The scene had all the signs of a robbery; groceries strewn across the floor, money from the cash drawer on the floor, and several extremely terrified people talking with state police outside. The only side effect to this theory was the fact that the police already had the perpetrators in custody.

When Alan asked what was going on, the answer only gave way to new questions that he wished he had the time to ask. Instead, he bit his tongue and asked the young woman who now stood behind the check out counter for directions to a house he knew only as *The Brunswick House.*

"You sure you wanna go up there mistah?" The young woman asked with a strong New England accent.

"Why? Is there something wrong with this place?" Alan asked.

"Well. . ." the woman began but then hesitated. Looking around the store several times and then outside three or four times, she finished. "It's haunted."

"What?" Alan asked in a bit of a chuckle.

"It's haunted; has been for years. No one dares go up there; especially after what happened to the last owner."

"What do you mean? What happened to the last owner?" Alan asked.

Again, the woman behind the register hesitated. . . looked around. . . and then said, "Mister Stevenson, Shane Stevenson, was the last owner. They say he died of a brain aneurysm but if you ask me. . ."An older woman walked in from outside and walked to the back of the store forcing the clerk to pause again.

"I think he was scared to death of being there. He frequented the store a lot and would tell every body about the ghosts he'd seen there. Most the people in town thought he was nuts, but not me." The young woman finally finished.

"And why is that?" Alan asked.

"I used to live up that way, about two houses down, before Mister Stevenson bought the place. I used to ride my bike up and down the road all the time. I always heard a lot of strange things going on up there."

"Like what?"

"Noises. . . but no one was living there."

"That could've been the wind."

"No, not like shudders slappin' against the house. . . more like screamin' and whalin' like someone was being killed or somethin'."

"And there was no one living there?"

"No."

"What happened there? Why was it abandoned before Mr. Stevenson bought it?"

"Years ago, two people were found murdered in that house; Tom and Annie Brunswick. They were found at the top of a staircase just inside the house. Their killer. . ."

The older woman from the back made her way to the end of the far aisle with a mop bucket. The young woman behind the counter lowered her voice to almost a whisper as she continued her story.

"Their killer was never found. There were signs that someone had possibly fallen down the stairs, but the couple was found at the top of the staircase. The detectives that investigated the scene, in their infinite wisdom, concluded that it had to have been the killer that had fallen down the stairs."

"Yeah, I know a few detectives like that." Alan said sarcastically.

"Anyway, after six months of investigations, they still had not found the killer or the murder weapon."

"You're kidding."

"They closed the case after another month of just sittin' around on their asses and filed it."

"That figures." Alan said. "Despite all of that, I still need to go up there. From what I understand, a friend of mine inherited the place from this Mr. Stevenson and I'm supposed to meet him there. I'm just not too familiar with Maine's coastal highways."

"Well, I'll tell you how to get there but please remember what I told you. The spirits around that house are extremely unpredictable." The young woman said as she began explaining in detail the directions to the house.

* * *

Stepping out of the store and walking over to one of Maine's finest on the scene, he flashed his identification and told them who he was.

"What can I do for you Sergeant?" The trooper said, looking at the badge and identification.

"Well, if you don't mind telling me; what happened here?"

"We had an attempted robbery here earlier." The trooper told Alan without a hint of accent.

"Did you get the name of the person who prevented the robbery?" Alan asked. "The reason I'm asking… I'm here on a special assignment to bring someone back to Atlanta. I think he might be the man who may have prevented this crime." Alan said.

"No, just a description," The trooper exclaimed.

"What's that?"

"Black man, late twenties early thirties, dressed all in black. A woman was with him; dark hair, petite. The clerk said that the woman looked like she had been through hell and back."

"The woman sounds familiar. Unfortunately, the man she was with her doesn't ring a bell. Any idea where they might've headed?"

"Well, the clerk said that an out-of-town woman was in earlier asking for directions. She said the woman had sort of a southern accent."

"Where was she asking to get to?"

"She was asking directions for the old Brunswick house. I'm kind of hoping that the clerk was wrong about the destination though."

"Why is that?"

"Well, if she *was* correct; that house is haunted. The stories of that house are synonymous around here." The trooper said.

"Don't tell me you believe this haunted house stuff." Alan said.

"If you've seen and heard what I have in all the years I've been on the force…"

"Well, not to sound criticizing Officer… Cookson; is it… I'm not really a believer in that kind of stuff. If you'd like, if I find this hero of yours, I'll send him your way." Alan said, returning to his rental car.

* * *

Ten minutes after pulling out of the store's parking area, Alan was driving through an open wrought-iron gate and up a long mud filled drive leading to a huge house. A sign at the front of the house stated that it was the very house in which he was looking for.

Peering through the windshield, desperate to avoid hitting anything; Alan drove slowly enough to avoid any falling debris from the trees as they swayed in the wind and rain. As if out of thin air, completely without warning; a large man began running at him from the direction of the side of the house with his fist in the air.

Slamming on the brakes to avoid hitting him, he came to a complete stop only about ten feet from the house. Getting out of the car, he looked around in the rain filled night but couldn't see anyone. There was absolutely nothing out there. Shaking his head in bafflement, Alan got back inside the car and drove the rest of the drive up the hill and parked along side another car sitting in front of the house.

"This must be their car." He said as he got back out of the car after killing the engine.

Climbing the steps to the house, he stepped up to the door and began to knock against the hard wood.

"**A**lan! What're you doin' here? No, don't tell me, let me guess. That sorry excuse for a detective still has a crush on me and he sent you to get me." Alex said, answering the door.

"Somethin' like that. But *'that sorry excuse for a detective'* doesn't know me very well. I intend to help you the best way I can. Hell, you don't think I'd turn down a vacation on the department, do ya?" Alan said.

"Well then... get on in here and outta that rain." Alex said, laughing and motioning Alan inside to join them.

"We've just been discussing everything that's been happening to us."

"That should make for an interesting story. Have you told anyone about the incident back home?" Alan asked.

"Not yet. Why; you wanting to hear it all over again?" Alex said.

"No, no, that's not what I'm saying. C'mon Alex, you've known me a long time. . ."

"Exactly, I also know you're a cop." Alex interrupted.

"Hey!I resemble that remark." Samantha said, coming out of the dining room to meet the new guest.

"Sgt. Alan Perkins, meet my sister Samantha Elliot, a detective with the Tulsa Police Department in Oklahoma." Alex said, giving introductions.

"Really... his sister... and a cop?" Alan said, shaking her hand. He then turned to Alex and said, "Look buddy, I'm on your side. I'm just trying to get all the facts so that I can clear your name and get Detective O'Grady off your back for good."

"You trying to tell me that son-of-a-bitch doesn't have any other suspects other than me?"

"What're you guys talkin' about?" Samantha said, interrupting again.

"Let me calm down a little and I'll explain."Alex said, motioning for the two of them to follow him back to the dining room.

After several minutes of silence after returning to the dining room table, Alex finally said, "I guess it's time for me to be totally honest with everyone."

Stephanie looked at him and asked him with only a look if he was sure of what he was doing. He answered with a nod.

"Alan, I really need you to stay seated for this." Alex said.

"Seated for what? What are you talking about?"

"Just listen…" Alex began, "When I arrived at Stephanie and Bridget's house, I hadn't really noticed anything out of the ordinary right away. Not until I came closer to the door… the living room was dark, but there was light coming from the hallway when I went inside. When I went to check out what was going on, I heard voices coming from Bridget's room… men's voices.

"To keep from being seen, I hugged the wall as I approached her room. When I looked inside, I saw two men in her room and then I saw Bridget tied to her own bed. She was beaten… bloody… her clothes were torn. I couldn't take it anymore."

"Are you telling me what I think you're telling me?" Alan interrupted.

"Please let me finish." Alex said. "I killed the two men that had done that to her. When I untied her, I sent her to the neighbor's house to call the police. I then went in search of Stephanie."

"I don't think I want to hear this, Alex. I can't help you if I know this."

"Alan, you're a good friend and you deserve to know the truth. Please let me tell you everything." Alex said protesting.

"Once Bridget was safely out of the house, I headed for Stephanie's room and found her in much the same way, only this time, the son-of-a-bitch attacking her wasn't just attacking her; he was trying to rape her. I pulled the guy off of her and threw him onto the floor. He went for his gun but I was quicker." Alex said, finishing his story.

Silence filled the room as they allowed the story to sink into their minds.

"Alex. . . I don't know what to say." Alan said, standing up from his seat and walking over to the sliding glass door at the back of the room.

With rain beating against the cemented patio outside, Alan stared blankly outside the glass.

"Why didn't you tell us the truth Alex?" Alan finally asked, turning to look at him.

"You know the answer to that question Alan. I did nothing wrong but that sorry excuse for a detective would've found a way to fry my ass." Alex said.

"Why didn't you at least tell me, instead of hopping a plane and heading up here?"

"I was going to tell you everything, but never got the chance. This thing here was a coincidence; I had to get these two away from all that and this came up at just the right time." Alex said as he stood and began making his way to his friend.

"So, now that you know, what're you gonna do?"

"I don't know yet man… but I won't let you fry for this. If I were in your shoes, I would've done the same thing."

"What about your job? Won't you lose your job if you're caught helping me?" Alex asked.

"Don't worry. I have an idea… an idea that will not only help you, but will save my job at the same time."

"What would that be?" Alex asked.

"I just won't find you."

"What?"

"Let me worry about it, old friend, I owe you that."

* * *

"Okay, now my turn to talk," Samantha said. "I agree with you Alex on one point, what happened in that house was not your fault. What I don't agree with is; it doesn't matter if this detective has a thing for you or not, if you were arrested for this, you could probably get off on a number of different technicalities."

"Like what?" Stephanie said, speaking up because she was the most worried about Alex getting in trouble.

"Obviously, a lack of physical evidence is a big one."

"What do mean 'lack of physical evidence'? His fingerprints were in the house."

"I didn't leave my fingerprints anywhere in the house that night… other than on your attackers." Alex said, interrupting.

"Was the gun that Alex used on the third man found?"

"No, that was…" Stephanie said as Alex interrupted her.

"That was lost." Alex said.

"Lost?" Alan said.

"Yeah… lost."

"I thought you were being honest here." Alan said.

"I didn't say that I didn't know where I left it. What I said was that it's lost."

"Well, back to what I was trying to say." Samantha said.

"So, what were you saying? You want me to turn myself in Sam?" Alex said.

"Well, in a way, yes. We can fix all of this by you turning yourself in, but at the same time, don't tell this detective what he wants to hear. He'll just turn everything you say around on you and nail you in the end. Make him do his job and figure it out on his own." Samantha tried to explain.

"I think I follow you," Alan said turning to Alex. "If we make O'Grady happy by you going back with me… cooperate with the investigation. . ."

"When he exhausts himself looking for evidence, you'll go free and he'll go nuts." Samantha said, finishing her though and Alan's statement at the same time.

"Makes sense, but I don't like jails." Alex said.

"Without physical evidence to hold you, they can't keep you. So, there'll be no jail." Samantha assured him.

"You sure?" Alex asked.

"She's right Alex, without some sort of physical evidence tying you to the scene, they can't hold you. Besides, I talked with your attorney, Clayton Green, and he assured me that he would represent you if you needed him." Alan said.

Turning back to the glass door, Alan peered into the rain filled darkness. Out of the corner of his left eye, he spotted movement in the rain.

"There's someone outside!" He shouted, pulling his gun from the holster on his hip and opening the sliding door.

"What?" Samantha said, pulling her own.

"There's someone outside!"Alan repeated. "Stay here! I'll find who it is."

"I'll go with you." Samantha said.

"No, I got it." Alan said.

"The hell you do! I said; I'm going with you!" Samantha shouted, following Alan with her own gun in hand and pointed down at her side.

CHAPTER 27

Thunder rumbled through clouds. Lightning jumped from one cloud to the next. The wind howled through the air as rain fell hard to the ground. Darkness enveloped what little light protruded from inside the house and overtook it quickly.

With his gun in both hands and outstretched in front of him Alan searched desperately through the backyard from one end to the other. Samantha, with her own gun, followed close behind with her back to Alan so as to monitor the opposite direction. They were determined to find whoever it was that he had seen poking around.

A sound of a snapping twig or stick came from the edge of the woods. Cautiously, Alan and Samantha made their way to the source of the sound. Looking left then right, they searched desperately for the origin but the cause of the noise eluded them.

The wind began picking up, blowing the rain into their faces and blurring their vision even more. "Let's head back!" Samantha shouted over the wind. "If there was someone out here, they're gonna have to find shelter as well. This storm's picking up something fierce."

"Alright! You're probably right, let's head back!" He said, following her back across the yard toward the sliding door.

*　*　*

Back inside, they found the dining room deserted. "Where'd they go?" Samantha asked, breaking the silence between them.

"Don't know," he said.

"Alex…!Stephanie. . . !Bridget. . . !KJ. . . !Where is everyone?" Samantha called out.

"In here!" A voice sounded from across the foyer.

Following the sound of the voice that sounded like Alex, they found all of them in the comforts of the living room furniture. "Why'd you move in here?" Samantha said.

"The girls didn't feel safe in the dining room anymore so KJ and I took them in here. Have a seat… KJ was just about to start where he left off earlier." Alex said.

"As I was trying to tell you earlier before your friend arrived, my place here can not be revealed yet. I told Bridget I would tell you all when the time is right. Right now, my friends, the time is not right." KJ said.

"What're you talkin' about?" Bridget said. "The time is right… you told us you would tell us and we demand to know the truth about you."

"All I can say is this… Death lives here; it is no longer coming… because we have come to it. There is an evil presence here outside this house and it wants in very badly. You have each brought with you your own baggage. You have revealed it this evening. The pure of heart will survive and triumph." KJ said as everyone looked at him still dumbfounded by what he was saying.

"What?" Alex finally said after several minutes of total silence. Shaking his head, trying to get his brain to wrap around the words that KJ had just said, Alex said, "I don't get it; I see your lips moving, I can hear the English language coming from them, but I still couldn't understand a word you just said."

"Listening is not the same thing as hearing." KJ said.

"Look, do you know how to speak in words that are anything other than riddles?" Alex said.

"Yes, but one must learn to listen with his mind, heart, and soul… not just his ears." KJ said.

"Huh?" Alex said. "Look, I may live in a big city but I'm still just a redneck. Could you please talk to us in a way we can understand?"

"In other words, my friend; when you can understand the words I speak, you will be able to understand the mystery you seek behind my presence here." KJ said.

"I give up!" Alex said, getting up and walking out of the room.

"Alex. . ." KJ said, following him into the foyer.

"What?" Alex said harshly.

"Look Alex, I am not trying to upset you. I will be straight with you. I am on a mission and it is classified until the situation has been resolved and diffused. I have been assigned to you and your friends. I have been sent here to not only help you but to protect you. I know that you once served in the military, so you know what *classified* means and what it entails.

"I must speak in riddles so that others do not figure out who I am and why I am here. Do you understand?" KJ said as he pulled Alex close to him so that no one else could hear what he had to say.

"Yeah, I understand. Should I ask how you know about my military background?" Alex said.

"No, I couldn't tell you if you did. As I said before, all will be revealed when the time is right." KJ said.

"Alright, you two, stop being so secretive and let's figure out our sleeping arrangements." Samantha said, coming out into the foyer to join them. "If KJ doesn't want to tell us anything, he doesn't have to. But when daybreak comes… KJ… you're going to have to leave."

"I'm afraid that I cannot." KJ said, returning to the living room.

"And why is that?" Samantha said.

"Because as many of you have already figured out; it is no coincidence that you found me when you did or that you picked me up. I am here for your protection."

"Then you're going to have to tell us what is going on." Samantha said.

"In time all will be rev-"

"Yes, I know, 'in time all will be revealed.'" Samantha said, interrupting.

"Yes." KJ said.

"Look, there's a lot going on here and I don't think it's safe for anyone to leave here until we figure this thing out." Alex said, coming back into the living room. "As far as sleeping arrangements are concerned, we can discuss it all we want but I don't think anyone's going to get any rest with whatever is out there."

"You're not talkin' about that guy your sister and I chased off; are you?" Alan said.

"I'm not sure. All I know is, there's something outside that no one can explain." Alex said.

"That's putting it mildly," Stephanie said. "I literally was fought over upstairs by two men who disappeared just as quickly as they appeared.

"What are you talkin' about?" Alan asked.

"You better sit down for this." Alex said.

* * *

After explaining to Alan all that had transpired in his absence, Alan sat on the edge of the couch with his mouth tightly shut and his eyes wide open.

"You expect me to believe that this house is haunted?" Alan finally said.

"Believe it… don't believe it… that's up to you." Alex said. "But that doesn't make it any less real."

"Those that believe only in physical things are in for more danger than they ever considered possible." KJ said.

"What do you mean by that?" Alan said defensively as he jumped to his feet to confront KJ face to face.

"Chill Alan. . . KJ's here to help, not disrespect. He always talks in riddles. That's just his way. No matter how annoying it is." Alex said sarcastically looking back at KJ who stood his ground.

From upstairs came an ear-piercing, glass-shattering scream that filled every room in the house and brought everyone else to their feet.

"What the hell was that?" Alan said, running into the foyer and to the staircase where the sound seemed to emanate.

At the foot of the stairs lay a small pool of blood once again. "What the hell is that?" Alan said, looking down at the blood.

"My guess would be blood." Alex said. "I've seen this before."

They all watched as the pool on the floor gradually began to grow in diameter. They followed the trail up the staircase first with their eyes and then with their legs until they came upon a site none of them wanted to see. At the head of the stairs lay a woman who had been savagely and mercifully torn to shreds by what could've only been a knife. A man stood over her unaware of the captive audience he had conjured up.

"What the hell is going on?" Alan asked perplexed at what he was seeing.

"I don't know, but we've been seeing bits and pieces of this little play all night." Alex told him.

"What you are seeing is called an echo…" KJ said as he stepped behind them both and looked up, watching the same gruesome play that the rest of them were watching this very minute.

The man with the knife quickly moved away from the body disappearing into the darkness. From the direction of the downstairs bathroom, they could hear running water when none had been audible before, then suddenly… it stopped. A man appeared out of the bathroom seconds later and began searching the downstairs foyer. He then turned and ran up the stairs where they watched as he cradled the young woman's head in his lap. He then disappeared as the knife wielding madman had earlier outside.

"I don't understand this; who are these people?" Alan asked.

"These people are Tom and Annie Brunswick. What we are witnessing are the last moments of their lives. It is what is called an echo of their life." KJ said, answering his question.

"I don't understand," Alan said. "Are you telling me that those people are dead?"

"Precisely my dear detective; you are witnessing their last days. You must do what no one else has been able to do over the past twenty plus years for these people… solve the mystery surrounding their deaths. Solve the mystery of the Brunswick house." KJ said.

Alex led the way up the staircase, careful to stay as close to the wall as possible so as not to step in the manifestation of blood on the steps. At the top, he caught a quick glimpse of the body of Annie Brunswick before she faded from sight. The pool of blood, that had been beneath her body, remained on the floor.

"What happened? " Alan asked.

"This part of the play has ended." KJ said. "If you want to see part two… Alex, will you show us the way?"

Opening the door to the master bedroom, he ushered them inside and shut the door behind them. From the experience that Stephanie had witnessed earlier; this would be where the second 'Act' would play out.

When all were assembled, as if on cue, Tom Brunswick appeared sprawled across the bed face down. As if rippling out of thin air, a bigger man appeared to one side of the bed wielding a knife.

"This is where he looked up at me… the man on the bed… Tom… this is where he looked at me." Stephanie whispered.

"He may have looked as though he were looking at you Stephanie, but I assure you; he did not see you." KJ said.

With quick steadfast motions, the man wielding the knife seemed to vanish… reappear… vanish… and reappear inching ever so closer to the bed until he stood over the body of Tom Brunswick. They watched as the man plunged the knife into Tom's side and then withdrew it for a second run.

Tom kicked his way off the bed and threw the man away from him with unbelievable quickness. He got up from the bed and began to run toward them only to vanish once more. The armed assailant got to his feet and followed close behind, disappearing just as Tom had done when he neared them.

"This is way too weird…" Alan said, watching with his mouth open wide in amazement at what he was witnessing.

"The events that played out in this house on the night of the Brunswick's deaths; the echo that you are witnessing will continue to play in sequence until we can solve this murder." KJ said.

"So, all we can really do is watch?" Bridget said, beginning to understand.

"Precisely…" KJ said, turning to face her.

Suddenly, from downstairs, a pounding sound echoed up to them. "What the hell was that?" Alan said, turning sharply in the direction of the noise.

"That would be the front door." Alex said, pushing past him to the stairwell.

The blood that had previously been at the head of the stairs had vanished just as the spirits had done earlier. Alex looked down the steps and found that the blood that had been trickling slowly down the steps had also disappeared. The insistent knocking at the front door continued vigorously. Shaking his head quickly side to side, trying desperately to release the images that he had seen there just moments before from his mind, Alex quickly moved past where he had seen the body of Annie Brunswick earlier and made his way down the stairs.

Approaching the front door, determined to see who it was pounding relentlessly, Alex reached for the knob just as a cold wind brushed against his arm. He started to turn the knob, only to have his hand yanked away from the door involuntarily.

"What the hell?" He said just as the others reached the bottom.

The pounding at the door stopped abruptly. Then from behind them, they heard a racket that sounded like someone falling down the stairs.

"I believe Act three has started without us." KJ said.

Rushing back to the stairs, Alex made it just in time to see the large man that had once wielded the knife come to a stop at the bottom of the stairs, cracking his neck on the wall as he landed. At the top of the stairs, they saw Tom Brunswick lift his wife's head from the floor and place it in his lap as he once again shimmered into the air and out of existence.

Looking back at the huge man lying at the bottom of the stairs, they watched in astonishment as he too disappeared.

"Is that it?" Stephanie said.

"I don't think so." Samantha said. "I remember seeing this guy outside. That's where he dropped the knife. So, I know that he didn't die inside the house."

"If he had… there wouldn't be much of a mystery to solve; would there?" Alan said sarcastically.

Bridget punched him in the arm.

"You know that's assaulting a police officer?" He said, looking at her as he rubbed his shoulder where she had punched him.

"You're a little out of your jurisdiction there." She retorted.

Suddenly from the direction of the kitchen, they heard a lot of commotion. Scurrying their way into the kitchen; they made it just in time to see the large man leaving through a wall.

"Wait a minute… how could he have done that if this is an echo? Wouldn't he have had to go through a door or something?" Alan said, pointing at the wall.

"There were a lot of renovations done to this house when our grandfather bought it. I'm certain there used to be a door where that wall is now. He probably put it in when he decided to put in the sliding glass door in the dining room. No sense in having two doors to the backyard so close together." Samantha said.

"That makes sense." Alex agreed.

"Quick… if we're going to see where he's going, we better get to the sliding door and follow him." Samantha said.

"I'm not going out there." Stephanie said.

"Alan and I will go." Samantha said, pulling her sidearm once more. "We're the ones with the guns; we should be the ones going out there."

"I don't think guns are going to do you much good." Bridget said. "If he's a ghost, it's not like you can hurt him."

Arriving at the sliding door, they peered out into the rain and found the large man swaying back and forth hunched over and holding his neck with his left hand.

"He's hurt pretty bad. I would just about bet the son-of-a-bitch died out in those woods." Bridget said, watching the killer step out of the openness of the backyard and into the dark confines of the woods behind the house.

"If he did, that would explain why no one has been able to find the body." Samantha said. "The one thing about Maine's woods is that they are thick. You could go for miles before you ever get out of them and it's really easy to get lost if you don't know your way around."

"I thought you were just a little girl when you moved out of Maine…"Stephanie said.

"I was, but my adoptive parents used to bring me up here every now and then so I would remember where I came from."

"Did you ever come and visit our grandfather?" Alex said.

"No… didn't really know where he was. We came up here a few summers while I was growing up. A friend of my adoptive mother's told her about Maine and how beautiful it was up here. We took the first vacation when I was ten and came up camping and fishing up here. The last time I was here was when I was fifteen. That time, we just visited some of the old towns and museums."

"Well, I guess there's only one way to see if that's where he is…" Alan said as he reached for the door to open it.

The lock on the door, which he had just unlatched, suddenly latched once again while he held the handle in his hand.

"What the hell?" Alan said as he unlatched the lock once more only to have it lock again. He pulled hard on the door handle a couple of times but then was pulled away from the door by some unknown source.

The others watched in amazement as Alan began to walk backwards away from the door, turning his head one way then the other, trying to figure out what or who had a hold of him.

From the front door came the insistent knocking once again. Alex quickly turned and ran toward the door determined to see who was playing games with them. As he reached the front door, he too was stopped dead in their tracks by someone or something holding onto him. Alex turned his head one way then the other just as Alan had done to see who or what had hold of him, when suddenly whatever had him let go. Alex began to walk toward the door just as Alan and the others came into the foyer from the dining room. Out of nowhere, the air in front of him began to ripple and then a man appeared in front of him. It was Tom Brunswick.

Holding a hand out in front of him to stop Alex, he said, "Please do not open this door."

Stunned at the sudden appearance of a man that had been dead for several years, he stood in silence staring at him. Stephanie broke Alex's hypnosis when she touched his arm as she cowered beside him. Alan who seemed to be stunned as well at the sight of this manifestation suddenly began to shiver in place as gooseflesh erupted across the skin of his arm and the back of his neck.

"Uh… KJ… could you come here please?" Alex finally said.

"I am right behind you, my friend." KJ said, putting his hand on Alex's shoulder.

"Uh… do you mind explaining this to me since you seem to know so much about what's going on?"

"Most certainly… as you can plainly see, this is Tom Brunswick."

"Please, cut to the gist of it." Bridget said, stepping up beside Stephanie as Samantha stood on the other side of Alan.

"Okay… what you saw before was an echo… a constant reenactment of a person's final moments on this plain of existence. What you are seeing now is the actual manifestation of Tom Brunswick." KJ explained.

"And this is supposed to explain everything *how* again?" Alan said.

"Maybe it would be better if I can explain it." Tom said, speaking up.

With all of their attention on Tom Brunswick now, he began to explain, "We've been trying for so long to get someone to pay attention to us… to see us… to help us. My wife and I were just about to give up until Shane Stevenson bought our house. Over the years, we've been trying to get people's attention by allowing them to see what happened to us but they just got scared and moved out. But Shane Stevenson did not.

"He watched with interest at our demise but when we tried to communicate with him; he couldn't see us. His mind was only open to the echo. He tried to speak to us and we could hear him but he had no way of knowing that. He said that he would find a way for us to rest in peace, but death took him from us before he had the chance to fulfill his promise."

"Well, if he couldn't see you… how is it that we can?" Samantha said.

"Because your minds have been open to the truth…" KJ said. "Samantha, your mind was opened when your partner began showing himself to you. Alex's mind became open when he began to see images of the man you had described to him that killed your partner..."

"Hey, wait a minute! I never told anyone about that. How did you know about it?" Alex interrupted.

"The same way that I know that before you met me on the side of that road that you had seen me before... in your dreams. Samantha had also seen me before as well..."KJ said.

"In the bar... you were the guy in the shadows." Samantha said, shaking her finger at KJ.

"Okay, now you're starting to freak me out." Alex said.

Suddenly, a woman appeared at Tom Brunswick's side. Without the trauma that they had seen her in earlier, they barely recognized this to be Annie Brunswick, Tom's wife, until he introduced her.

"This is my wife, Annie..."Tom said as he put his arm around her waist and stepped away from the front door.

"I apologize Sgt. Perkins for..." Annie said as Alan interrupted her.

"How did you know my name?" Alan said, then turned to KJ, "How did she know my name?"

"I've been listening and watching you all since you arrived in this house." Annie said.

"So, what were you sorry for? Spying on me?"

"No, I was apologizing for pulling you away from the door... I did not mean to scare you."

"You didn't." Alan lied.

"Wait a minute... you still haven't answered my question here KJ." Alex said.

"What *was* the question, Alex?"

"How is it that *you* know all of this?"

"My friends... I believe it is time that I reveal my true self to you all. Please, let us retire to either the dining room or the living room." KJ said.

Taking a seat at the dining room table, they each sat in silence as KJ began to tell his story.

ust as his story was beginning, KJ was interrupted once more by the sound of the howling wind outside. They tried to ignore it but then something drew Stephanie's attention to the glass door. When she looked in its direction, she screamed and jumped in surprise.

Standing outside the door, untouched by the rain, stood the malevolent specter of the Brunswick's killer. He stood outside the door staring in at them. He didn't say anything or try to communicate in any way. He just stood there. Silent.

"Holy shit!" Alan shouted in surprise. "Where the hell did he come from?"

Getting up from the table, Alex approached the door. The man outside looked like he was breathing hard in anticipation of what he was going to do if Alex decided to open the door. But he couldn't have been *actually* breathing… could he?He was dead… wasn't he?

Getting closer to the door; mesmerized at the sight of this huge man standing outside like a boogeyman in a child's room waiting behind the closet door for the light to go out, Alex reached for the handle intending to open it and confront the monster. His hand was jerked away from the handle, but this time not by one of the spirits within the house, but by his own sister.

The monster continued to stare in through the glass. His eyes were intense and full of rage. His hulking shoulders heaved up and down with false breathing and with his right fist, began pounding on the glass door slow and steady.

"He wants you to let him in." Samantha said, turning Alex toward her. "We can't play his game."

"You're right… we've got to figure out how to get rid of him." Alex said, turning away from the angry specter outside.

"KJ, we still want to know your secret, but maybe you're right for now… maybe it is too soon to know everything about you. But since you do know more about this kind of stuff than we do, what do you think we should do?"

"He is angry for what happened to him. He wants revenge on the man that killed him, even though he already killed him as well." KJ began. "We need to give the Brunswick's peace. The only way to do that, I'm afraid, is to do something the police in their time could not do. We must solve the secret of the Brunswick House; we must identify their killer and ensure that the authorities here close this cold case."

"Okay, and how do you plan we do that?" Alan asked skeptically.

"We find his body."

"They've got to be bones or dust by now." Alex said.

"Bones… yes; dust… no, not quite yet." KJ said as if he knew something they didn't.

"If we find the killer's body. . . , are you sure that would that set their souls free?" Samantha asked.

"If his remains were turned over to the authorities here and identified… I'm one hundred percent sure that they would be able to move on." KJ said.

"Then we need to decide on who's going and who's staying." Alex said. "We know from the echo we've all witnessed, that the killer went through the backyard and into the woods. So, I figure…"

"His body's in the woods somewhere." Samantha said, finishing his thought.

"Okay, who's going and who's staying?" Alex asked.

With the proverbial straws drawn, it was decided that Alex, KJ, and Samantha be the group to look for the remains of the unknown Brunswick killer. Alan would stay with Stephanie and Bridget inside the house to provide a distraction. The spirits of Tom and Annie Brunswick agreed to aid in their plan only so that they could finally have peace.

With Alex and his small reconnaissance group waiting patiently at the sliding door, peering into the rain swept darkness, Alan and the girls took positions at the front door. The plan was for Alan to distract the evil spirit toward the front of the house long enough for Alex, KJ, and Samantha to sneak through the backyard and into the woods.

"He's searching the backyard; he must think his knife is out there." Samantha said.

"Alright… I'm goin'!" Alan shouted from the front door.

"Alright, get ready guys." Alex said, looking at KJ and Samantha as he grabbed the handle to the sliding door.

Within the silence of the house, they could hear the front door open and then close a second later. "He's out!" Stephanie called out.

In a matter of seconds, after hearing Stephanie tell them that Alan was outside, they watched as the killer looked up sharply from the ground toward the side of the house and then fade away.

"Now!" Samantha said, urging Alex to hurry.

Opening the door and slipping into the rain with KJ bringing up the rear, they raced into the woods. Suddenly, Alex realized that he had forgotten a most important tool for their expedition; flashlights.

"We will not need them." KJ said as he came up from the rear of the group to take the lead.

* * *

Alan found it difficult to see in the front of the house, not only because of the rain falling so hard, but also because of the pitch darkness that the tall Maine trees surrounding the house provided.

Suddenly, the wind began to blow from all different directions all at one time then stopped abruptly. From out of nowhere, came a sudden shove to his chest. He felt as if he had just been speared by a huge football player as he was lifted off his feet and sent flying backward nearly ten feet, landing hard against the ground.

"What the. . . ?" Alan said, trying to pick himself up from the ground. Without warning, he was lifted into the air, as if he were nothing but a pebble, by an invisible and powerful being only to be slammed hard once again to the ground.

Trying to pick himself up from the ground once more, a quick succession of phantom kicks pelted into Alan's chest and gut from his unseen assailant. Drawing breaths as best he could; he managed to muster out one single word in the form of a screamed whisper… "Help!"

With no possible way of hearing him, Bridget suddenly appeared in the doorway and ran into the rain toward him. "No…"He tried to say, knowing that the monster would target her next. Unfortunately, there was no strength left in him in order to make his scream heard.

Bridget grabbed hold of his forearms and began pulling him across the ground until she could lift him to his feet. The outside light suddenly lit up the night and they could clearly see the silhouette of his assailant in the mist of the rain then suddenly, the man creature began charging toward them.

Another arm grabbed him and he was pulled to his feet as both girls lifted him and took his weight on to themselves, pulling him onto the porch. The killer was approaching fast but within only another second, they were once again inside the house and the door was safely shut behind them.

"Son-of-a-bitch... son-of-a-bitch!What the hell *was* that?" Alan cried out, gripping his ribs and grimacing at the sharp pain shooting through his chest.

The second that the door closed and was secured behind them, the specter began pounding on the door once again with an insistent... persistent... and annoying constant pounding.

* * *

"What do mean we won't need them?" Alex asked as he followed KJ deeper into the woods.

"I have excellent night vision; we won't need flashlights. Besides, with the spirit of the killer out here among us, we don't need to give ourselves away."

"He's right," Samantha agreed. "If we use flashlights, we might as well shoot up a flare and lead him right to us."

"Yeah; but won't he sense us?" Alex said.

"If Alan was able to stall him this long, he's probably got that spook so pissed off right now; he's not focused on anything else." Samantha said.

"And his hesitance would benefit us even greater." KJ added.

Five hundred yards from the house and deeper into the woods, they cautiously traveled through the rain, wind, and trees. Six hundred yards now, KJ stopped... frozen in place. With darkness surrounding them, Alex didn't see him stop and nearly busted his nose open against KJ's skull as he walked right into the back of KJ's head.

Samantha, on the other hand, did see him stop and had to put her hand over her mouth to muffle the laugh that tried to escape her when she saw Alex holding his nose and constantly checking his hand to see if his nose was bleeding.

"What's wrong?" Alex asked, rubbing the tenderness away from his nose.

"Listen. . ." KJ said.

"All I hear is the wind and rain." He said after remaining silent for a minute.

"Wait. . ." KJ said and moments later the rain stopped and the wind fell silent. "Look. . ." KJ said, pointing ahead.

Baffled by the sudden stop of the rain, but more so by the fact that KJ knew it was going to, Alex looked in the direction he was pointing and found that only about a hundred yards away, against a tree, lay the figure of a corpse wiped clean of everything but its tattered clothing and bones.

"Is that what I think it is?" Alex asked.

"What?" Samantha said, coming up from the rear to get a better look.

"Yes, it is… there lays the remains of the Brunswick's killer." KJ said.

* * *

Sucking in the pain and slowly getting to his feet, Alan pulled his gun from his shoulder holster and began making his way back toward the door. Vengeance shined in his eyes.

"What're you gonna do Alan, shoot him?" Bridget remarked sarcastically as she tried to stop him.

"I've never let anyone treat me like that, I'm not about to start now." Alan said, standing erect.

"Alan, I know you better than anyone… You know that." Bridget said. "This is something you can't fight. You can't kill this thing; it's already dead. Alex will find a way to stop it."

"That's all the more reason to go out there. If for no other reason than to make sure that thing doesn't go after them. I know there's history between us Bridget… but you know me, I can't stay here and do nothing with a friend in danger."Alan said.

"Leave the gun here." Bridget said stubbornly.

"I'll be defenseless!" Alan exclaimed.

"What defense can a gun bring you against a ghost?" Bridget asked. "He could take that away from you and you couldn't do a thing about it."

"Leave it Alan, for all our sakes." Stephanie agreed.

"Alright. . . alright, you win. You're right; a gun's not much good against someone that I can't see." He finally relented.

Relinquishing the gun and holster to Bridget, he said, "Just keep an eye on me and help me if you can. If you can't do anything to help me… if it looks like it's going to kill me… shoot me before that thing can do anything. Promise me…"

"I can't do that." Bridget said, taking the gun and holster in hand.

Ignoring her comment, probably hoping that she would do it anyway, Alan opened the door and stepped out onto the porch. The rain suddenly stopped and silence surrounded him. Nothing whatsoever was making a noise. No rain… no wind… nothing.

Suddenly, coming from his right, Alan felt a sudden gust of wind and then felt two massive hands wrap around his neck and heave him into the air. Struggling to get free, Alan hit at his assailant trying to loosen himself from those massive invisible arms, but it was no use.

His breathing became labored and he could slowly feel the world growing dark all around him. He knew he was slipping into a state of unconsciousness. He knew that would be dangerous, because he would be unaware of what the killer would do next. Maybe that would be a good thing.

Darkness enveloped him from all sides and finally overtook him within seconds. Closing his eyes, he gave into it.

CHAPTER 31

"You know. . . for a corpse that has been out in the woods this long – among the elements, among wildlife, and such – the skeleton seems quite preserved. The bones are all intact, his clothes are a little raggedy but they're still hanging off of him." Samantha whispered observing the corpse.

"You know something… you're right. This guy's been dead for some time, animals surely would've taken away some of the bones… torn at the clothing… something. This doesn't make any sense." Alex agreed in a low but audible whisper.

"Animals are afraid to come this close to the body." KJ said.

"What do you mean?" Alex said.

"As long as the killer's spirit roams these woods and the perimeter of the house; no animal will dare come close enough to his body." KJ said.

"But what about the crows we saw coming up the driveway?" Alex asked.

"The crow is the messenger of death; it symbolizes that death *lives* here. With each caw the crow sounds, it gives a new message. One only has to listen in order to understand." KJ said.

"There you go again, talking in riddles. Just once, I'd love it if you gave a straight answer." Alex said, getting upset but keeping his anger subdued to a whisper.

"That would not be my way, my friend. If you were told everything, you would learn nothing. If I give you clues and you figure them out, you become a wiser man." KJ said.

"No, if you told me straight out what I want to know when I want to know it, you'd keep me from getting a headache trying to figure you out and my patience wouldn't wear so damn thin." Alex said.

"Patience is a virtue; wisdom is a gift. Think about what I tell you and you will know what I'm talking about." KJ said.

"Forget it, I'll figure it out soon enough." Alex said. "Let's gather these up and get back to the house before it figures out where we are."

* * *

Bridget had wasted little time to pull Alan's unconscious body back inside the house. When his invisible assailant finally dropped him to the ground, she ran outside and grabbed hold of him. With strength she was unaware she possessed; she lifted him from the ground, threw his arm around her neck as his feet dangled against the ground, and dragged him inside the house.

When the door was shut, the relentless pounding started again almost immediately. Stephanie locked the door both to prevent the creature from somehow getting inside as well as to keep Alan in *if* he managed to regain consciousness.

"What're you doing?" Bridget asked.

"Makin' sure this damn fool doesn't get himself killed when he comes to." Stephanie said.

"He's done his job," Bridget said, holding Alan's head in her lap. "There's no need for him to go back out there. Now it's up to Alex and the others."

"But what if that thing goes after them?" Stephanie asked worriedly.

"Don't worry Steph… those three are more than capable of handling themselves." Bridget said reassuringly.

"That doesn't stop me from worrying, ya know."

"I know… just think… as long as that thing's bangin' on the front door, it hasn't sensed them in the back." Bridget said.

The pounding continued. *BAM!BAM!BAM!*

Then silence.

* * *

Shrugging out of his long dark overcoat, KJ laid it across the ground offering it as a way to transport the skeletal remains. As Samantha kept watch, Alex and KJ quickly gathered each piece of crucial evidence and placed them in the coat. When that task was complete, Alex gathered the tattered clothing and placed them atop the bones. KJ wrapped his coat around the collection and tied the sleeves tight around the bundle so that nothing could escape and lifted the make-shift bag from the ground.

Just as he flung the bag of goodies over his shoulder, as though he were some demented Santa getting ready for Halloween trip rather than a Christmas Eve one, the wind outside began to pick up into a howl. It seemed to come from all different directions at once. As suddenly as it had begun, the wind stopped, leaving with it, the appearance of the specter of the Brunswick's killer.

Appearing at least fifty yards away and the opposite side of the tree in which his corpse had been laying against, the killer began to vigorously walk their direction. The faster they seemed to be getting away from the poltergeist, the faster he seemed to be gaining.

It did not run but walked solemnly and with purpose as it quickly gained on them. When they reached the sliding door, the killer reached out his huge hand in order to grab one of them but KJ sensed him. Pivoting quickly around to face the beast, KJ spoke in a language that none of the others could understand and caused the specter to turn to dust and fall to the ground only an arm's length from him.

"What the hell was that?" Alex said as KJ closed the door behind them.

"That was the killer of the Brunswick's." KJ said, trying to forego the true answer Alex was looking for.

"You know what I mean..." Alex said as he was interrupted by Stephanie running into the dining room when she heard them enter the house once more.

"Alex!"

Looking away from KJ to see what was going on, he said, "What is it? What's wrong?"

"It's Alan..."

"What happened to Alan?" Alex asked as he followed her to the front door.

"Alan? Oh my God… what happened?" He said when he saw Bridget sitting in the middle of the floor with Alan's head in her lap.

"That thing out there attacked and nearly killed him." Bridget said, looking up at him with tears streaming down her face.

Alex had never seen her like this. Bridget was normal pretty tough… normally the one that would hold it together regardless of what happened around her. She had when they had been attacked in her home. She had been frightened sure… who wouldn't have been? But after Alex rescued her, she pulled herself together and remained strong for Stephanie. She had been Stephanie's rock for years; long before Alex had ever come along.

"Is he hurt bad?" Alex asked.

"He's hurt bad enough," she said. "Did you find him? Did you find the killer's body?"

"The remains no longer rest in the forested grave, but rather now in the darkness of my coat." KJ said, solemnly turning in place so that both women could see the coat over his shoulder was in fact full.

"Now what?" Bridget said, wiping the tears from her eyes with one hand.

"Now, we get these bones to a forensics lab. I don't suppose any of you know where the closest one might be." Samantha said.

"There is a forensics lab at the Maine State Police Headquarters in Augusta," KJ said.

"How do you know that?" Alex asked.

"I know many things, Alex. Now is not the time to reveal them." KJ said, starting to sound more and more like a broken record.

"If you know so much… What's this guy's name so we can put an end to this right now?" Bridget said hatefully.

"Your anger is understandable Bridget, but you should not direct it at me. What I know about the circumstances here is limited. With what I do know, I can only aid you in searching for the answers. This mystery is yours to solve. I am here simply to make sure that you are not harmed in the mean time." KJ said.

"Well, I think you're falling down on your job there, pal," Bridget said still annoyed and angry. "In case you're not paying attention, Alan isn't doing so great."

"I am deeply sorrowed for this mishap, but even I cannot prevent everything. I can do what I can to make sure it does not happen again though. I will accompany whoever is going to Augusta to make sure that they get there safely." KJ said.

"And what about the rest of us?" Stephanie said before Bridget could.

"You should be safe inside the house. Unless you let it in, evil cannot cross that threshold without being invited in." KJ said as he made his way to the front door.

"Well, considering that Alan's hurt and I'm the only other law enforcement officer here, I suppose I should go." Samantha said.

"I will stay with Stephanie and Bridget and help them take care of Alan." Alex said.

"How long has he been like this Bridget?" Alex asked, looking down at his long-time friend.

"A good twenty minutes now. That thing out there was waiting for him to come back out." Bridget said, looking back down at Alan resting in her lap. "If I hadn't pulled him in here, that thing would've surely killed him."

"Well, I guess we better get started if we're going to solve this thing before anyone else gets hurt." Samantha said.

* * *

As Samantha and KJ were about to open the front door, Alan sat straight up from the floor shouting one single word. "NO!"

Stopping dead in their tracks, they each turned to face Alan as he collapsed again to the floor but when Samantha went to turn the doorknob, the insistent pounding returned, yet this time from the back sliding glass door in the dining room.

"Good; now's our chance. Let's go." Samantha said, opening the door and leading the way outside and to the rental car.

* * *

"Let's get Alan to a more comfortable place girls," Alex said, reaching down to pick Alan up from the floor.

"Where? All the bedrooms are upstairs; he's not exactly a lightweight." Bridget said, getting to her feet once Alex had Alan hanging safely over his shoulder.

"He'll be more comfortable upstairs." Alex said.

"Well, I'm sure he's real comfortable right now thrown over your shoulder." Bridget remarked sarcastically.

"Are you sayin' my shoulders aren't comfortable?" Alex joked.

"Uh. . . let me think about that. Yes!" Bridget joked in return, trying to lighten her mood once more.

"He'll never know; he's unconscious." Alex said.

"Yes, he will. Cause I'll tell him." Bridget retorted.

"That's okay. I'll just tell him it was your idea." Alex said, climbing the stairs to the second floor.

"I'll deny it." Bridget said, following Stephanie and Alex up the stairs.

"I'm glad to see you back to your old self." Alex said.

In the bedroom next to the one in which he and Stephanie had claimed for their own, Alex laid Alan carefully down onto the mattress. After ensuring that Alan was comfortably beneath the covers, he and Stephanie started to leave the room when they noticed that Bridget was not following.

"What's wrong?" Stephanie said.

"I'll watch him." Bridget said insistent on being left alone with him. She pulled one of the reading chairs closer to the bed and sat down.

"I had a feeling you would." Alex said.

During most of the trip from Rockport to Augusta along Highway 17, neither Samantha nor KJ spoke much to one another. Not that she didn't have a ton of questions to ask, because she did, she just didn't have any idea how to start a question-and-answer conversation with him and keep it from turning into some kind of interrogation.

Within an hour, they stopped at a traffic light at the end of their drive on 17 and had a choice of only two directions to go – right or left.

"So… Which way?" She said, turning to face her silent passenger.

"Turn left… the state police headquarters building isn't far." KJ said.

Sure enough, within only a couple of minutes after making the turn, she found the building on the right side of the road. Pulling into the half moon drive, she parked the car and switched off the engine.

"I don't know how you know the things you know," she finally began, "but I wish that you would tell me something."

"I have told you everything that I know to tell you." KJ said.

"I don't think you have, but I'm not going to argue with you. Let's go on inside and find some answers." She said, opening her car door and stepping out.

The night sky was cloudless in this part of the state. They had actually driven out of the cloud cover more than fifteen minutes earlier. She was certain that it probably wouldn't be much longer before the storm made it this far inland though.

With KJ following close behind, carrying the skeletal remains they wished to have identified, Samantha entered the red bricked building and went to the window provided for them, in which an older fairly out of shape woman sat behind the dispatcher's station with a headset phone system wrapped over her head.

"Can I help you?" She said as she looked up from her computer screen.

"Yes, my name is Detective Samantha Elliot. I'm with the Tulsa Police Department in Oklahoma." Samantha said, holding out her department issued ID case containing her badge and identification card complete with picture, rank, division, and date of hire.

"Could I speak with the ranking officer in charge tonight? It's of the utmost importance."

"Just a moment ma'am; I'll have someone out to speak with you shortly." The woman said.

* * *

They had been sitting in the small waiting area for only about five minutes when a door opened just to the left of where KJ was sitting. A tall rather thin man stepped into the room wearing Captain's insignia bars on his lapel.

"Detective Elliot?" He said, holding the door open.

Getting up from her chair she looked at KJ and said, "Wait here. I'll be right back."

The captain led her through the door and into an office at the end of the hall. "What can I do for you Detective?" He asked as he opened the door to his office, allowing her to go inside.

Taking a seat in a chair across from a desk she looked up at him and said, "Well, to make a long story short, my brother, some friends, and I stumbled upon some skeletal remains of a body within the woods behind a house that my brother and I just inherited from our recently deceased grandfather."

"I'm sorry to hear about your grandfather. Are you sure the bones you found were human?"

"I've never seen very many animals wearing clothes Captain…"

"Day… Captain Robert Day," he said. "Where are the bones now? They still at the site?"

"No, my friend outside has them in his overcoat along with the clothing that it was wearing. I have reason to believe that it belongs to a man… a very bad man."

"And what reason would that be?" He asked.

"Because of where we found them… the house is actually quite famous along the coastal towns. I don't know whether or not the legend made it this far but…"

"Oh, I don't know. I've been around quite a long time as you can see by my graying beard and hair. Where is this house?"

"It's the old Brunswick house just past the town of Rockport."

"Did you just say… the Brunswick House?" He asked, sitting back in his seat in total surprise at the name she had given him.

"Yes, I did," she said. "Do you know it?"

"I think everyone in the police force here in Maine has heard the stories of that house and the weird things that happens up there."

"Well, I also found this…"She said, pulling the handkerchief wrapped knife from her jacket pocket.

Retrieving a latex glove from the pouch of his duty belt, he picked up the knife and brought it close to him for a better view. "Where did you say you found this in conjunction with the house?"

"The knife, I found in the backyard about fifty yards or so from the house. The remains, we found approximately seven hundred yards from the house deep in the backwoods."

"*The Brunswick House* murders have never been solved ya see…" Captain Day started to explain. "The killer was never found. Every cop in this state would give anything to be the person to solve that one. Hell, they even put it on *Unsolved Mysteries* once about a year or so ago. Had a lot of tourists wanting to stop by and take a look at it but the owner – your grandfather – wouldn't let anyone in. He put up a gate at the entrance to the driveway to keep people out."

"Well, if I'm right, and I'm almost certain that I am, then the remains we found this evening are probably of the killer," she said.

"Well, you came to the right place Detective. We have the best forensic specialist in all of New England employed at this very precinct. Let me get him in here." Captain Day said, picking up the receiver.

"Beth, could you see if you can get Jeff McFarland on the phone? Tell him it's crucial that I speak with him."

"Do you think he'll be able to identify the remains?" Samantha asked.

"Jeff McFarland is the best like I said. If anyone can do it… he can."

Within only a couple of minutes, his phone rang and based on the expression and the sound of the captain's voice, she could tell that McFarland had to be the person on the other end of the line.

* * *

"Bob, what're you calling me up for this late at night? What's so damn important?"

"I said crucial, not important. How would you like to be the guy to solve the biggest unsolved mystery in Maine's history?" Captain Day asked.

"What mystery?"

"*The Brunswick House.*"

"You have my attention."

"I have a detective here from Oklahoma who claims she has inherited the house from her grandfather. She says that, while checking out the property with her brother, she stumbled across some skeletal remains of what might be the unknown killer of Tom and Annie Brunswick."

"You're kiddin' me."

"No, I'm not. She says she has the remains here. She also brought in a knife she found, which may have been the murder weapon."

"I'll be there in twenty minutes." Jeff said, hanging up the phone.

* * *

Within exactly twenty minutes, Jeff McFarland rushed into the office of Captain Robert Day.

"What'd you do, speed?" Captain Day said.

"No, look at what time it is genius, there's no one on the road at this time of night." Jeff joked.

"Hello…"Jeff said, looking over at Samantha who had turned in her chair to look at him. "I'm Jeff McFarland. You must be the detective Bob was talking about."

"Detective Samantha Elliot." She said, standing from her seat and shaking his hand.

"Here's the knife Jeff." Captain Day said, picking up the knife again and handing it to him.

Pulling a pair of latex surgical gloves out of his right front pocket and slipping them on, Jeff took hold of the handle and stared intently over each and every inch of the knife. "There's definitely dried blood on the blade here, along with rust from the weather." Jeff said, pointing at different sections of the blade.

"How can you know all of that from just looking at it?" Samantha said.

"Because he's good." Captain Day said before Jeff could say anything.

"I'll prove it once we get to my lab. Bob said something about you finding some remains…"Jeff said.

"Yes, my friend outside has them." Samantha said.

"You mean that rather dark and spooky looking gentleman in the waiting area?"

"Yeah, that'd be him," she said.

"By all means, let's head over to my lab and find out who this mystery man is then." Jeff said, leading Samantha out of the office and outside to another building that had the name *Maine State Forensics Lab* on the side. Following close behind them once they appeared through the door to leave station, KJ carried the bag of remains over his shoulder.

A full hour had passed before Alan regained consciousness. When he opened his eyes, he saw Bridget sitting at his bedside watching him diligently.

"How long have I been out?" He asked in a whisper.

"At least an hour… can I get you anything?"

"Yeah, the tag number on that truck that hit me."

"I only wish it was that simple. I do have some good news though."

"Really. . . what's that?" Alan said, trying to sit up.

"Be careful; you got bruised up pretty good there."

"Tell me about it. What's the good news?"

"They did it… they found the son-of-a-bitch… they found his bones in the woods."

"Where is everyone?" He said, trying to look around.

"Samantha and KJ took the bones to a police crime lab. Alex and Stephanie are waiting downstairs."

"Does that mean that thing out there is gone?" Alan asked, ignoring Bridget's comment of being careful and sitting up in the bed.

"Wish I could say yes, but that damn thing hasn't stopped pounding on the doors yet. It's been going from the front door to the back door and back again every five minutes."

Using the bed sheet for leverage, Alan began pulling himself to the edge of the bed, determined to get out of it. "Where do you think you're goin'?" Bridget asked, getting up from her chair to stop him.

"I can't stay in this bed; I'll go nuts."

"Oh yes you can old friend," Alex said from the doorway, "you need your rest. Besides, you're already nuts."

"Alex, I'm no good if I'm lying around in bed," Alan tried to argue. "You know that."

"You're no good if you don't let your body mend a little before you try to break it some more either. So, stay in bed and rest yourself. Besides, if you don't, Bridget will most likely hurt you worse that that thing out there ever thought about."

With Bridget looking at him with the sternest look she could muster, he said, "Okay, okay, you win. I'll try and get some rest, but if anything happens – and I mean anything – you better not leave me up here." Alan reluctantly conceded.

"Deal… now get some rest," Alex agreed. "Bridget, are you gonna stay up here?"

"Somebody's gotta take care of him," Bridget said. "He's too damn stubborn for anyone else to handle."

"Okay; Stephanie and I will be downstairs if you need us." Alex said as he left the doorway and headed back downstairs.

*　*　*

"Is he gonna be alright?" Stephanie asked when Alex met her back in the hallway by the head of the stairs.

"Eventually… as long as he stays in that bed and gets the rest he needs." Alex said.

Returning to the dining room, Alex nearly walked into the spirit of Tom Brunswick who had suddenly appeared in the doorway. "Jesus!" Alex said in surprise.

Annie appeared at Tom's side. She had a concerned look on her face. The pounding continued at the front door as Tom said, "What happens now?"

"Now, we try and hold off that asshole out there until my sister and our new found friend gets back here." Alex said.

"What if they can't find out who he is? We're going to be stuck here forever." Annie said.

"Samantha will find out who he is…" Alex said. "She has to."

Suddenly, the pounding stopped.

* * *

Bridget waited for Alan to fall asleep and when he finally did, she got up from her seat determined to go across the hall to the bathroom. As she quietly stepped into the hallway, he felt a cool and gentle breeze blow through the hall from the direction of a window at the opposite end of the hallway from the staircase.

Deciding that she could hold it a little while longer, she started toward the window to investigate when she saw shards of glass scattered across the floor. "What the…"She whispered just as she felt a force push against her torso, slamming her back against the right-side wall.

When the pressure left her chest, she tried to pull herself away from the wall. Then, as though, she was as light as a feather, she was lifted into the air and held there for several seconds. Violently, seconds later, she was slammed back to the floor. Before she could even attempt to get her breath back, she was shoved by the unseen force across the floor until she collided with the banister at the head of the staircase.

Darkness overtook her quickly and she closed her eyes to it.

* * *

A loud noise from outside his room woke Alan from his minimal amount of slumber. "What the hell was that?" He said as he pulled himself carefully up again. "Bridget…? Bridget?"

Slowly pulling himself out of the bed, Alan stumbled his way to the door, and while holding onto the door jam, peered into the hallway. There, he found Bridget lying motionless against the banister at the head of the stairs.

"Bridget!" Alan shouted as he dragged himself into the hallway determined to reach her despite the agonizing pain he was having in his chest, stomach, and back.

Suddenly, from behind him, he felt something grab him and hoist him into the air. *Oh no, not again!* He thought when his feet left the ground. Like a mischievous little boy wanting to break a toy to get his parents' attention, he was slammed hard against the wall repeatedly until consciousness left him and the pain he had been feeling previously suddenly disappeared.

* * *

After hearing a lot of banging and thumping coming from upstairs, Alex quickly made his way to the staircase. From upstairs he heard Alan shouting for Bridget. Hurrying up the stairs, he could hear more thumping coming from the hallway.

Before he even noticed Bridget lying motionless beside the banister, he became witness to Alan being slammed repeatedly from one wall to another like a pinball. When whatever it was that had a hold of him was done, it dropped him to the floor where Alan lay motionless.

"Alan… No!" Alex shouted, moving to his fallen friend's side.

Suddenly, a gust of wind erupted through the hallway as a window in one of the bedrooms across the hall shattered completely. Alex checked drastically for a pulse against Alan's neck, but couldn't find one. Dropping his head to his chest, he felt the warm tears streaming from eyes and down his cheeks.

"NO!" Alex screamed.

"So… let's check this knife out first off." J eff said, taking the knife from Samantha. He walked over to a work station that contained a microscope, a computer, a fingerprint analyzing machine, and other forensic equipment that Samantha knew very little about.

Taking a scalpel from a drawer and a new pair of gloves from a box, Jeff began to slowly and carefully scrape bits of brick-reddish almost brown crust off of the edge of the blade. Putting that little chip of material into a test tube, he then placed about a quarter inch of liquid inside the tube. From there, he took the tube over to another machine, put it inside and turned it on.

"Okay… this looks interesting and everything, but what exactly are you doing?" Samantha said, watching him closely.

"I'm determining whether or not the substance on this knife *is* what I said it is."

"Okay, then what?"

"Well, if you would have your friend bring those skeletal remains you found over here to this long table, we can sort through them and try to put together the skeleton."

"That should not be too difficult." KJ said, bringing the coat filled with bones over to the table indicated and opened it up.

Looking over the remains, Jeff finally began handling and reconstructing the skeleton piece by piece as though he were a child again, reconstructing a puzzle. After nearly fifteen minutes of working on the skeletal puzzle, he finally stepped away from the table and marveled at his work.

"Wow... I can't believe you did that so fast." Samantha said, marveling at this genius of science.

"Well, you're definitely correct in assuming that it was once the body of a man. The..." Jeff started to explain in detail how he could tell the skeleton belonged to a man but Samantha stopped him.

"Mr. McFarland, I would love to hear you explain how you know that this was once a man but I'm afraid that we don't really have that much time. What we would like to know, as I'm sure everyone in New England would as well, is who he is."

"Well, I might be able to take some impressions of his teeth and run it through our systems but if he never visited a dentist, that won't do much good."

"Is there another way you might be able to determine his identity?"

"If there was some kind of DNA sample I could take, I might be able to but the likelihood of getting a strong enough sample of the bones is pretty rare."

"What about from his clothing?" KJ said, speaking up.

"If there is anything left on the clothes, I might... but given the amount of time that this body had to have been in the woods and at the mercy of the elements, it's not very likely that I'll get anything from that either."

"How long do you think it will take?" Samantha said, picking back up on the questioning.

"If everything works in our favor, probably five or six hours." Jeff said.

"Good."

"But it could also take a lot longer if things aren't in our favor." Jeff objected.

"Well, my faith is in everything *being* in our favor Mr. McFarland." Samantha said.

*   *   *

Nearly an hour passed while Jeff McFarland worked on the evidence before him. Samantha stood nearby observing him with great curiosity. KJ had decided to go outside and wait.

About five minutes past the hour, KJ came back inside the lab and grabbed Samantha by the arm, pulling her close to him. "May I speak with you privately?"

"Sure." She said, telling Jeff McFarland that she would be right back.

Once outside, she looked at KJ as he looked across the street at a tree. "What's up?"

"We need to get back to the house. I feel something very tragic has happened to one of the others back there." KJ said very seriously as he turned to face her.

"Do you know what's happened or to whom?" She asked.

"No, but as you can see in the tree behind me; a solitary crow remains in one tree where the others have moved across the road." KJ explained.

Looking past him at the tree across the street, she saw the single crow he was talking about and then in the tree on their side of the street, she saw three other crows perched in it.

"Okay, I see the crows… but what does that have to do with everyone back at the house?"

"Death has come for that one." KJ said, pointing to the single crow across the street. "You see… the crow signifies both life and death. It is the carrier of souls from this plain to the next. When a person dies, a single crow will separate from the rest and wait for the soul to exit the body before taking off to carry it to judgment."

"You know; I get that you're a little… eccentric… but how do you know all this?"

"I am the keeper of the crows."

"What's wrong Alex?" Stephanie shouted as she began to make her way up the stairs.

"Stay down there sweetheart; don't come up here."

"Why? What's going on?"

"Just please… stay down stairs." Alex begged, wiping the liquid that was coming from both his eyes and his nose. "I'll be down in a minute."

"Okay Alex." Stephanie agreed, knowing that Alex was trying to protect her from something.

Getting up from his friend's side, he went over to Bridget and felt her neck for a pulse. He found one; though it was weak. He picked her up from the floor and carried her downstairs to where he found Stephanie waiting impatiently at the bottom.

"What happened?" Stephanie said as fear began to mangle her voice.

"Get some cold water. I'm going to lay her on the couch." He said, taking the final step and turning to his left to go into the living room.

Stephanie returned a minute later with a glass of cold water and handed it to him. He brought her over to kneel beside Bridget and gave the glass back to her. "Try to get her to take small sips. Raise her head a bit and put the water to her lips. Don't lower her head until you're sure that the water has gone all the way down. Wait five minutes and do it again until she regains consciousness." He explained.

"What's going on?"

"Alan's dead. I've got to go take care of him. I don't want you to leave her side."

"What's happening?"

"That thing… that thing is trying to get in. It managed to break a window upstairs and killed Alan and nearly killed Bridget too. I've got to board them up. I'll be back soon."

"Don't leave me!" Stephanie shouted, getting up from the floor and throwing her arms around his neck.

"You'll be safe down here," he said. "The Brunswick's are down here and they'll let you know if that thing is coming."

"How do you know that?"

"Just trust me sweetie… will you do that?" He said, trying to get loose from her so he could do what he knew needed to be done.

Finally releasing him, she returned to Bridget's side and did as he had instructed. Alex ran back up the stairs and into the very room in which he had laid Alan's unconscious body only a couple of hours ago. Tearing the sheet from the bed, he went back into the hallway and draped it over his fallen friend.

Just as he was getting back to his feet, he felt something grab his shoulder. He wheeled around and found himself staring directly into the eyes of death itself, manifested into the spirit of the yet unnamed Brunswick killer.

"Put him down you bastard. It's me you want… not him." A voice said from behind the phantasm.

Turning his head in the direction of the voice, Alex saw the manifestation of Tom Brunswick standing directly behind them. The phantom killer held Alex in the air reasoning with itself on whether or not he wanted to succumb to Tom's suggestion for several minutes. Finally, he decided; sending Alex to the floor with a loud *THUD* as the air was knocked out of him.

"Get out of here!" Tom shouted to Alex. Alex wasted little time at all as he quickly ran down the stairs.

* * *

From outside the front door came a furious non-stop pounding once again. "He did it!" Alex said aloud as he reached the bottom of the staircase.

Joining Stephanie in the living room once more, Alex told her of what he had encountered upstairs. She was as surprised as he was that the Brunswick's would protect them as they had.

"I don't think they want any more blood shed in this house." Alex said.

Stephanie couldn't take the insistent pounding on the front door any longer. It was completely driving her mad. She got up from Bridget's side and ran to the door screaming, "What do you want? What do you want?"

The pounding suddenly stopped and total silence filled the foyer. They listened closely as they made their way to the front door. As they grew closer, the voice grew louder from a low gravely whisper to a roar. "I. . . want. . . you. . . all. . . to... DIE!"

Suddenly, all the windows in the house began to vibrate and the insatiable pounding began again on the front door and echoed throughout the house. With each bang against the door came a single word accompanying it, "DIE!"

After conferring with Jeff McFarland about what they needed to do, he assured them that he would find a way to let them know his findings. Samantha and KJ returned to the rental car and spared little time getting it back on the road. When they were on Highway 17 and nearing the town sign, she turned to him and said, "What did you mean when you said you were 'the keeper of the crows'?"

"It's much too difficult to explain." KJ said, trying to get out of answering the question.

"Try!" she said. "And no more of these damn riddles. It's just you and me in this car and I'm not about to play games with you."

"Okay okay. . . I never realized how dominating you can be," he said. "Look, this is going to be really hard to understand but I need you to keep an open. . ."

"I'm pulling over." Samantha interrupted.

"Okay. . . I suppose there's no easy way to put this… I'm not of this plain of existence," he said.

"I said no riddles," she said as she began to apply the brakes.

"I assure you… no riddles. What I say is true. To make it easier for you to understand, let me explain it like this…"

"I'm listening," she said.

"I'm sort of… a guardian angel in a sense. I was sent here to help the Brunswick's find peace by assisting you in finding their killer and giving them closure on their deaths."

"Okay, call me crazy, but I believe you. But you still haven't answered my question."

"What's that?"

"What did you mean when you said you were 'the keeper of the crows'?"

"Each guardian is granted dominion over certain creatures that have been blessed by God. You see the creatures of the world were created without what God knew man would fall victim to – free will. He blessed each creature with gifts that would allow a guardian to utilize in order to watch over his charges."

"So, you're telling me that you were sent here by God to help us and that you use crows as like a familiar or something." She said, trying to grasp what he was telling her.

"In a way… yes. There is much more to it than that simple of an answer but I suppose that it the bottom line."

"So, you're saying that you're a guardian angel…"

"Well… in a sense. I'm not really an angel… just a Guardian. I was once a part of this plain of existence but my life was cut short at the age you see me now. I'm really not supposed to reveal any of this to anyone… but I feel that if I do not, my mission will fail."

"Your secret is safe with me." She assured him.

"Thank you, my friend."

"So, what do we do now?"

"We get back to the house before this killing spirit can do any more harm." KJ said.

The drive during their conversation was remarkably short. Within only another half hour, they were driving up the muddy driveway to the Brunswick house. From above the top story of the house, they noticed a single crow circling in the air; it was barely visible in the night sky but dawn was fast approaching over the horizon giving enough light to shine its eyes. Several others were perched on top of the roof of the porch cawing into the wind.

"What the hell is this all about?" Samantha asked.

"It means; we need to hurry." KJ said.

A softer knock sounded at the front door followed by a familiar voice, "Alex, it's me. Open the door."

A little reluctant for fear it might be a trick, Alex opened the front door and found Samantha and KJ standing outside. "Hurry up. . . get in here." He demanded, waving them inside and quickly shutting the door behind them. "I have some terrible news. . ."

"Sgt. Perkins is dead." KJ responded before Alex could tell them his news.

"Yeah. . . wait a minute. . . how did you know that?" Alex said, looking at KJ in surprise.

"I can sense though, that his soul is still here among us." KJ said, making his way to the staircase.

"Wait! How did you know about Alan?" Alex shouted.

No response.

"KJ; don't ignore me!" Alex shouted again, only this time, following him to the stairwell.

"He tried to intervene when the killer began to attack Bridget upon entering the house. The killer turned his attention to Sgt. Perkins and killed him by smashing him against the walls of the hallway. He then attacked *you* Alex, but stopped before he could do any damage; allowing you to go free and to help Bridget. He then escaped through one the bedroom windows as you descended the stairs." KJ said, telling the story word for word and play for play as if he had been there when it happened.

"Can you even hear me?" Alex said, standing to one side of KJ and looking directly at him.

"Yes, Alex, I can hear you." KJ responded without looking back in his direction.

"Then how the hell do you know all of this?" Alex repeated in a more demanding tone.

"It is a long and strangely understandable story, trust me." Samantha interrupted.

"I'm not going anywhere; I'd really love to hear it; no matter how bizarre it may be." Alex said.

"Just remember you said that." Samantha said.

* * *

"Okay, you're right, it is strange *but* believable." Alex said when KJ finished his tale. "So, if you know all this, why don't you just tell us the killer's name so these people can find peace?"

"Because there are some things I do not know and or not allowed to say." KJ said.

"Which is it? You don't know his name or not allowed to say?" Alex asked.

"By telling you what I've already told you is more than I should have, but it was unpreventable. Unfortunately, all I can do is watch over you and make sure you are protected while you solve this mystery from this point on. Alex, what you do for these people will show what you're truly made of and earn you a chance to make everything right in your own life." KJ said.

"What're you saying KJ? What do you mean?" Alex asked.

Suddenly the pounding returned at the front door; more insistent now than before; consistent and forceful. The pounding grew stronger and louder for several more minutes, and then suddenly stopped.

"You... will... all... DIE!" The strange and raspy voice swore from outside the door.

Shaken by the voice coming from beyond the door, Samantha said, "What the hell was that?"

"That was our friendly *'let's get along with everybody'* ghost outside demanding our heads." Alex said.

"Since when does he talk?" Samantha asked.

"Oh, I'd say about ten or fifteen minutes before you got here; he's been whailin' like that for a while." Alex said.

"Have you tried communicating?" Samantha asked.

"Oh yeah; that's when he started this *"I'm going to kill you all"* crap," he said.

"Well, he killed Alan…" Stephanie said, emerging from the living room. "So, I wouldn't take him too lightly."

"If we all stick together, we'll be fine." Alex said, trying to reassure them all. "Only when we're separated are we a target."

From behind them, the front door flew open as a large gust of wind blew through. Turning their attention to the door, they saw a huge man standing about six-foot-three in the doorway. He had huge shoulders and a barrel chest. The clothes he wore somewhat resembled the jumpsuit in which they had found in the woods earlier. Embroidered above his left breast pocket were the numbers *00654.*

* * *

As the stranger made his way into the foyer, another gust of wind blew through. This wind, however, originated from within the house and was coming from the staircase. A moment later, Alan Perkins appeared between the evil entity in the doorway and them.

"Alan?" Alex said, alarmed at the sudden appearance of his recently deceased friend.

Ignoring Alex's stunned response to his appearance, Alan stood firmly in front of the evil being trying to enter the house and shouted, "You can't hurt me anymore you evil son-of-a-bitch! No more disappearing acts."

Suddenly, but without a windy entrance, another figure took form along side Samantha on her right. With the sudden appearance of someone beside her, Samantha turned and found the gentle face of her former partner Dan Riley.   Without a single word spoken, he joined the spirit of Alan in front of the nameless killer and together began to force him back outside. When the door slammed shut behind them, all but KJ looked at one another in bewilderment.

Suddenly, the door flew open once more. Dan Riley appeared in the entrance with a glum look on his face. Beside him appeared the spirit of Alan Perkins with a look of sadness on his face. Before any of them could fathom what was wrong, the specter of evil appeared behind them both and then lifted them in the air in front of him. With unbelievable strength, the creature threw both men across the room, literally through Alex, Samantha, and KJ who were standing the closest to them.

"You can't hurt me you fools. I'm bigger and stronger than you. My power is unparallel. I will have my vengeance and you all… will… Die!" The killer said as he stepped through the door and into the foyer.

Stretching his arms out to his side, palms open and facing the evil spirit before him, KJ seemed to have had enough. In an ancient language that nobody listening could understand, KJ said, *"Shi'cA waNz^I uN he!"* (Be gone evil one)

With an unseen force, the huge mammoth was catapulted off his feet and thrown out of the doorway, beyond the porch, and onto the ground outside. The door slammed shut behind him. Letting his arms slowly fall back to his side, KJ turned to face everyone.

"What the hell just happened?" Alex asked baffled.

"A temporary measure until we can get the answers we need." KJ said. "I told you that I would protect you until you can solve this mystery."

* * *

"Dan? What are you doin' here?" Samantha said, coming to the side of her fallen friend who came to a rest in the dining room.

"This evil is getting stronger Kid." He said as he stood from the floor. "You need to solve this case or it'll destroy all of you."

Even as Samantha was looking into the eyes of her former partner, before she could say anything at all, the air around Dan began to ripple before her eyes and Dan faded out of sight.

* * *

"Alan?" Bridget said from behind them, standing in the doorway of the living room just as Alan was pulling himself from the floor less than a few feet from her.

"How can this be?" She said, approaching him.

Turning to face her, Alan held out his hand to her. She reached for him but their hands never touched. Instead, hers went through his. With tears streaming down her face, she said, "Alan…?"

"There's something I always wanted to tell you but was always too scare to say it." Alan said, coming face to face with her.

With tears still streaming her face, she said, "Don't…"

"I love you, Bridget. I always have. I wish things could've been different between us." Alan said as he faded before her eyes.

With an outstretched hand, Bridget reached for Alan to come back to her but he could not. Stephanie laid her hand on her shoulder and Bridget turned to her. Without any word spoken, she threw her arms around her friend's neck and they held each other tight.

* * *

When the noise outside had finally diminished and everyone had managed to finally relax, they retired into the dining room once more where Samantha began to explain what little they had learned in Augusta. She assured them all, however, that she had every confidence in Jeff McFarland and that he would be able to get to the bottom of this mystery.

"So, how is this Jeff McFarland supposed to contact us to let us know what he's found?" Alex asked.

"He's either going to come over here himself or send a patrol car over to let us know his findings." Samantha said.

"That's a pretty far drive… what makes you think he's willing to travel that far?"

"The fact that this mystery has gone unsolved for a number of years; everyone wants to be the one to solve it, and he seems quite tenacious about being the one to do it. Apparently, it would make his career." Samantha said.

"And how long is this investigation supposed to take?" Stephanie asked.

"Well, it could take a while," Samantha said, "but with this being one of the most famous unsolved mysteries in this state and he being a forensic scientist desperate to solve it; it could very well take mere hours."

"Problem is, depending on how old that skeleton is; will there be any medical records to compare to?" Alex said.

"Well, there is some good news to that. It seems that our mystery man had been a former guest of this state's prison system. A reluctant and discontented guest obviously. The clothes he was wearing when we found him turns out to be prison issued." Samantha said.

"And being a prisoner; he would have medical records still on file. Even as an escapee, they'll be buried somewhere." Alex said, getting gist where she was going with her answer.

"Exactly…" Samantha agreed.

"And we're supposed to just sit here and wait for this McFarland guy to bring us this information?" Stephanie questioned.

"If we had a computer terminal here with Internet access, I would be able to correspond with him that way, unfortunately, our late grandfather thought of a lot to leave us with, except the things we'd need to solve this mystery." Samantha said

"Yeah, no kidding; I'd kill for a phone right now." Stephanie said.

"Well, I could go back and see if I can help him out." Samantha said almost too eagerly.

"We'd still be waiting here to find out the results while that thing out there continues to try and get in here to kill someone else." Stephanie said.

Alex quickly responded before anyone else could talk. "Actually, Sam, that's not a bad idea. But I think you should take the girls with you. I'd feel safer."

"Are you sure?" Stephanie asked.

"Yeah, I think it would be best if you and Bridget went with Samantha and got as far away from here as possible." Alex said. "KJ and I will stay here and provide a distraction for you to get out."

Opening wide as if to tease them; the door slammed shut again at his suggestion and they all looked at it in bafflement. "What the. . . ?"Alex said as he reached for the front door knob to open it.

Alex pulled and tugged on the handle trying to open it but it wouldn't budge. It was if it had been locked from the outside but there was no lock to engage from that side. Getting frustrated, he shouted, "What the hell?" and kicked the door.

As if the kick actually had something behind it, the door flew open and Alex stepped onto the porch in time to see two silhouettes struggling as they rounded the side of the house toward the backyard.

"I don't know what's going on, but I'm not lookin' a gift horse in the mouth." Samantha said, looking beyond Alex's shoulder. Motioning for Stephanie and Bridget to follow, she headed for the car.

CHAPTER 38

Finishing his examination of the skeletal remains and the blood found on the knife that had been brought to him only hours earlier, Jeff McFarland began typing his findings into the database of his computer.

When that task completed, he began searching through files of the police databases, cross-referencing unsolved murders and escaped non-captured prisoners from the Maine State Prison, using no set years and within a three-hundred-mile radius of the prison. Surprisingly, he found what he was looking for; he quickly printed out his findings and picked up the phone.

"Hello?" A sleepy voice said, answering the phone.

"Mr. Shepard?" Jeff said.

"Yes."

"Mr. Shepard, this is Jeff McFarland; I'm with the Augusta Crime Lab. I need to get a hold of some prisoner medical files that have probably been sealed due to the length of time." Jeff said.

"What are you talking about?" Commissioner of Corrections Jay Shepard asked as he sat up in his bed, slowly waking up.

"I have reason to believe that a former convict of the Maine State Prison escaped some years ago." Jeff said. "I also have reason to believe that he brutally murdered a couple on the outskirts of Rockport. I would like to get your permission to review this man's medical file to compare DNA from the files and from some DNA found at the victim's home earlier this evening."

"Of course. . . of course, but we haven't had a successful escape from custody in years and those that have, didn't stay out long before they were recaptured. Any idea how long ago this incident took place?" Commissioner Shepard said.

"Well, I don't believe this one was ever captured. I'd say anywhere between twenty to twenty-five years ago."

Silence fell across the phone as Commissioner Shepard slowly began to ask, "What murders are you pertaining to Mr. McFarland?"

"*The Brunswick House* murders."

* * *

It took less than an hour to get all of the necessary information he needed faxed to him. After quickly reviewing and comparing, he grabbed all the paperwork and headed out the door and to his car.

Within an hour, Jeff arrived in Rockport. Following the directions given to him by Captain Bob Day, he pulled into the driveway to the Brunswick house. As he was pulling in, he noticed a car coming down the muddy driveway, trying to leave.

Honking his horn to get the driver's attention to stop; he was certain that the driver of the other car was Detective Samantha Elliot. He backed his car out of the driveway to give the driver room. The car pulled parallel to his and the driver rolled down the window.

"We were just coming to see you." Samantha said, rolling her window down.

"I did it!I solved the mystery of the Brunswick House." Jeff said excitedly.

"Follow me up to the house." Samantha said as she rolled her window up and put her car in reverse, backing all the way up the driveway and parking once more in front of the house. He pulled in behind her and parked but noticed that neither she nor her passengers had departed the vehicle.

Wondering if maybe she was waiting on him, he started to open his car door when she suddenly honked her car horn twice. Closing his door and deciding to wait to see what she was going to do, he sat quietly behind the wheel.

The front door opened and she flashed her headlights twice. A second later, a man exited the house and waved them inside. When the occupants of the car stepped out, Jeff followed as they quickly ran inside the house. He had read all the reports about this house but as of yet never been to or inside it.

With the door shut behind them, the man ushered them all to the dining room. Jeff introduced himself to each of the people who now gathered round the table.

With the formalities now out of the way, Jeff began to explain what he had found out. "This was just too exciting to send a message. I had to bring it to you myself. The samples I took from the knife did indeed turn out to be blood; the blood of Tom and Annie Brunswick. I ran a check on their marriage license and they had taken a blood test. That's how I was able to cross-reference the samples to be sure who it belonged to. The bones, however, were a little more difficult…"

"What do you mean; more difficult?" Stephanie said.

"Well, because the bones were so old and completely clean of any meat, it was very difficult to gather any DNA samples from them. However, I did find a few hairs on the clothes that you brought me. A couple belonged to Annie Brunswick, a few belonged to Tom Brunswick, but I was lucky enough to find some on the shoulders of the jumpsuit that belonged to our killer.

"I cross-referenced the DNA with those of escaped prisoners that were still at large, that the good Commissioner of Corrections was able to give me, and I found a match. About twenty-five years ago, a prisoner by the name of Jacob Frost escaped from custody after serving five years of a life sentence for the rape and murder of two women in the Kennebec County area. He had taken a guard hostage in order to leave the grounds. The police found the body of the guard shortly after they were called on the Brunswick murders.

"The police believed that Jacob Frost might have been the culprit behind the brutal murders of those two but they couldn't find any evidence linking them other than where they found the truck that Jacob Frost had stolen and stuffed the body of the guard in. The truck was just a little under a mile from the entrance to the Brunswick House but there was nothing inside proving that he had killed them."

"What about the knife wounds?" Stephanie said.

"The guard wasn't killed with a knife. He was killed with a make-shift weapon that in prison terms is called a 'shank'. After that night, Jacob Frost disappeared without a trace; until tonight. The Brunswick's killer. . . was. . . Jacob Frost." Jeff said.

Appearing just inside the foyer of the kitchen, a man and woman stood with hands clenched in one another and smiles across their faces. Jeff was somewhat taken back by what he was witnessing and he stood from his seat nearly stumbling out of it as he said, "What the. . . ?"

"Relax Mr. McFarland… meet Tom and Annie Brunswick, or should I say the spirits of Tom and Annie Brunswick." Alex said.

"This isn't possible." Jeff said opening and closing his eyes in disbelief.

"I assure you Mr. McFarland; they are the manifestations of the souls of Tom and Annie Brunswick and now that you have revealed the name of their killer, they can now truly rest in peace." KJ said as he turned to them and began speaking in that unknown language once again in a low but still audible voice.

As he spoke, he walked over to the sliding glass door and opened it. From outside the door, two crows flew inside the house and began circling above the heads of Tom and Annie Brunswick.

"What the hell are you doin'?" Stephanie cried out when he opened the door.

A glow appeared around both Tom and Annie. They then began to become less and less visible. They said their final good-byes as they turned into two radiant lights which flowed into the birds as they flew back outside the very door that KJ had entered.

"Okay, what the hell was that?" Jeff asked startled at what he had just witnessed.

"Mr. McFarland, please do not be afraid." KJ said, closing the doors behind his winged friends.

Jeff quickly began backing his way toward the dining room exit saying, "Look, you can keep what I brought you. I can print more copies for my own when I get back to the lab, but I can see things are way too weird around here for me."

"Jeff wait," Samantha said, running after him.

With a force compared to that of a powerful storm, the front door pulled off its hinges and away from the house. It was sent flying across the yard where it landed less than a few feet in front of Samantha's rental car.

"Oh Shit!" Samantha shouted as she pulled Jeff back into the dining hall. "Our friend's back."

"Who…? What are you talking about?" Jeff asked.

"There are a few things I neglected to tell you when we met." Samantha said.

"A few?" Jeff exclaimed.

"I'll tell you later," Samantha said, "I promise; but we need to move now."

"Alright girls, take Mr. McFarland upstairs and stay there until I come get you." Alex said as he and KJ provided a distraction.

* * *

Seconds after the girls and Jeff McFarland were safely upstairs; the spirit of Jacob Frost appeared inside the doorway.

"Now you will all die!" He bellowed in his raspy gravelly voice.

"I don't think so…"Alex shouted. "We know who you are Jacob Frost. It's time that you pay the price for your crime. Get 'em KJ!"

KJ stood silently beside him.

"KJ…?" Alex said.

"*K - J*…?" Alex repeated looking at him still motionless but staring back at him.

"You're not getting him." He mumbled through clenched teeth.

"I am sorry Alex; this battle is yours to fight." KJ said.

"What?" Alex asked forcefully.

"This is your third and final task in order to be free. You must figure this out for yourself and accomplish it without my assistance." KJ said.

"Thanks buddy." Alex said, sarcastically.

Turning his attention back to the poltergeist of Jacob Frost he said, "Alright asshole, let's see what ya got."

Walking across the room toward the door with more purpose than he had ever walked with in his life, Alex was determined to take care of this monster once and for all. But, as quickly as he had appeared, the spirit of Jacob Frost disappeared once again.

Alex stopped and began looking around, wondering what had just happened when he was suddenly picked up into the air once again as if he were a child's play toy.

"Put me down you son-of-a-bitch! You can't hurt me. You're a ghost, a spirit, a spook, nothing but hot air. Your identity has been revealed, your victims have been freed, your remains as I speak are no longer where you left them but are being cremated and dumped like an ashtray into the garbage. You have no reason to haunt here anymore." Alex shouted at the entity still holding him high above the ground.

"You cannot destroy *me* so easily…" Jacob Frost said.

"Don't get me wrong," Alex said, trying to squirm out of his grip. "If I have to, I'll give my own life… my soul… right now to see you… burn… in… HELL!"

"No need my friend, you have proven yourself." KJ said, raising his arms in the air and said, *"Shi'cA waNz^I uN he."*

From high above, a crow appeared, flying toward the doorway and then inside the house. The creature dropped Alex to the floor with a THUD. As Alex picked himself up from the floor, he watched as KJ stepped passed him and out onto the front porch where the crow was cawing at the killer, forcing him to back away.

A second later, a bright burst of light shone through the house. Alex had to cover his eyes to keep from behind blinded. When he opened his eyes, Alex saw KJ still standing on the front porch.

Without turning to face him, KJ said, "Jacob Frost will no longer bother anyone on this plain. He now sits in a long awaited judgment."

"Where are you goin'?" Alex asked, getting to his feet as he watched KJ descend the steps outside.

"My work is finished here. You know what to do now. Good luck my friend." He said as he walked into the fast-growing shadows the trees gave off as the morning sun began to rise in the horizon.

Alex ran after him but as he neared where the shadows of the trees began, KJ was gone.

CHAPTER 39

After assuring everyone that it was safe and normal again; they returned downstairs only to find the spirits of Alan Perkins and Dan Riley awaiting them in the foyer.

"Kid, you're gonna be okay." Dan said, looking at Samantha placing both hands on her shoulders and faded one last time from sight.

"I know I am partner; I know I am." She said, closing her eyes as a single tear ran down her face. She kissed her index and middle fingers of her right hand and held them up in front of her, saying her final goodbye.

"Alex, don't worry about O'Grady, he has nothing to go on. Without a confession from you, all he has is a robbery gone wrong. He'll think of something to cover his ass." Alan said, standing before his friend.

Turning to face Bridget, Alan said, "Bridget… thank you for being there for me. Know that I will always be there for you." He said as he too faded away into the mist before her eyes.

Tears began to flow down her cheeks and Stephanie quickly embraced her saying, "I know… I know."

"Come on guys, let's go home." Alex said. "Sam, I don't know about you, but I think we should leave the house the way it is."

"What. . . Close it down?" Samantha said.

"Unless you want to live here?"

"Let's close it down."

Turning to a still bewildered Jeff McFarland, she took his hand and shook it saying, "Thank you Jeff, for everything."

Staring at one another for a few minutes and then sharing a small amount of small talk; mainly because Jeff really wanted to know what was going on, they began to finally descend the outside porch steps, leaving the house wide open to all the elements.

"What're we going to do about the door?" Samantha said, following Alex, Stephanie, and Bridget outside.

"I'll pay someone to come up and fix it." Alex said.

* * *

Jeff McFarland called the Knox County Police Department to remove Alan Perkins' body from the house. Being the State Medical Examiner as well as the "best damn Forensic scientist in New England" as Captain Day had mentioned before, he ruled Alan Perkins' death an accident. Because the truth was too unbelievable, he reported that Alan had fallen down the stairs.

Alex paid to have the front door placed back onto the house and paid to have Alan Perkins' body sent home to Atlanta. Upon arriving in Atlanta, himself, he insisted on paying for the funeral of his friend and relented to Detective O'Grady's continuous questioning.

After a few months and no evidence supporting any of his allegations was ever found, O'Grady was left no other option but to drop the investigation against Alex and pursue other cases. He was quick, however, to start another investigation of Alex as to his involvement in the untimely "accidental" death of Sgt. Alan Perkins. It too was dropped after a couple of weeks. Thereafter, Detective O'Grady was reassigned to another department in another city.

Alex and Stephanie married within a year after their return from Maine. Bridget agreed to be the maid of honor; Alex insisted that his best man, regardless of his absence, was Alan Perkins.

Samantha, after speaking with her Captain, transferred to the Augusta Police Department within five weeks of returning to Tulsa, Oklahoma. She used her inheritance to buy some land and a house just on the outskirts of Augusta. She began dating a single Jeff McFarland exclusively for over a year and a half. He purposed to her on the anniversary of the day they met and hey were married one year later.

KJ Crow disappeared just as mysteriously as he had appeared.